JACQUELINE
☆ WILSON'S
Double Decker

www.jacquelinewilson.co.uk

Also available by Jacqueline Wilson:

Available from Corgi Pups, for younger readers:
THE DINOSAUR'S PACKED LUNCH
THE MONSTER STORY-TELLER

Available from Doubleday/Corgi Yearling Books:
LIZZIE ZIPMOUTH
SLEEPOVERS

Available from Doubleday/Corgi Yearling Books:
BAD GIRLS
THE BED AND BREAKFAST STAR
BEST FRIENDS
BURIED ALIVE!
THE CAT MUMMY
CLIFFHANGER
THE DARE GAME
THE DIAMOND GIRLS
DOUBLE ACT
GLUBBSLYME
THE ILLUSTRATED MUM
THE LOTTIE PROJECT
MIDNIGHT
THE MUM-MINDER
THE STORY OF TRACY BEAKER
THE SUITCASE KID
VICKY ANGEL
THE WORRY WEBSITE

Collections:
THE JACQUELINE WILSON COLLECTION
includes THE STORY OF TRACY BEAKER *and*
THE BED AND BREAKFAST STAR

JACQUELINE WILSON'S BISCUIT BARREL
includes CLIFFHANGER *and* BURIED ALIVE

JACQUELINE WILSON'S SUPERSTARS
includes THE SUITCASE KID and THE LOTTIE PROJECT

THE JACQUELINE WILSON DIARY
THE JACQUELINE WILSON ADDRESS BOOK
THE JACQUELINE WILSON JOURNAL

Available from Doubleday/Corgi Books, for older readers:
DUSTBIN BABY
GIRLS IN LOVE
GIRLS UNDER PRESSURE
GIRLS OUT LATE
GIRLS IN TEARS
LOLA ROSE

JACQUELINE WILSON'S
Double Decker

☆ DOUBLE ACT

BAD GIRLS ☆

Illustrated by Nick Sharratt

CORGI YEARLING BOOKS

JACQUELINE WILSON DOUBLE DECKER
A CORGI YEARLING BOOK : 9780440864141

PRINTING HISTORY
This collection first published in Corgi Yearling, 1998

19 20 18

Copyright © Jacqueline Wilson, 1998

including

DOUBLE ACT
Doubleday edition published 1995
Reprinted 1995 (twice), 1996
Corgi Yearling edition published 1996
Reprinted 1996 (four times), 1997 (three times), 1998 (twice)
Copyright © Jacqueline Wilson, 1995
Illustrations © Nick Sharratt and Sue Heap, 1995

BAD GIRLS
Doubleday edition published 1996
Reprinted 1996
Corgi Yearling edition published 1997
Reprinted 1997 (four times), 1998 (three times)

The right of Jacqueline Wilson to be identified as the
author of this work has been asserted in accordance with
the Copyright, Designs and Patents Act 1988

Condition of Sale

This book is sold subject to the condition that it shall not,
by way of trade or otherwise, be lent, re-sold, hired out or
otherwise circulated without the publisher's prior consent
in any form of binding or cover other than that in which
it is published and without a similar condition including
this condition being imposed on the subsequent purchaser.

Corgi Yearling Books are published by Random House Children's Books,
61–63 Uxbridge Road, London W5 5SA,
A Random House Group Company.

Addresses for companies within The Random House Group Limited
can be found at: www.randomhouse.co.uk/offices.htm

The Random House Group Limited supports The Forest Stewardship
Council (FSC), the leading international forest certification organisation.
All our titles that are printed on Greenpeace approved FSC certified paper
carry the FSC logo. Our paper procurement policy can be found at:
www.rbooks.co.uk/environment.

Printed and bound in Great Britain by
CPI Cox & Wyman, Reading, RG1 8EX.

www.kidsatrandomhouse.co.uk

Double Act

Jacqueline Wilson

Ruby illustrated by
Nick Sharratt

Garnet illustrated by
Sue Heap

CORGI YEARLING BOOKS

For Anne, Derek, Thorne and Franca Dorothy

ONE

We're twins. I'm Ruby. She's Garnet.

We're identical. There's very few people who can tell us apart. Well, until we start talking. I tend to go on and on. Garnet is much quieter.

That's because I can't get a word in edgeways.

We are exactly the same height and weight. I eat a bit more than Garnet. I love sweets, and I like salty things too. I once ate thirteen packets of crisps in one day. All salt-and-vinegar flavour. I love lots of salt and vinegar on chips too. Chips are my special weakness. I go munch munch munch gulp and they're gone. So then I have to snaffle some of Garnet's. She doesn't mind.

Yes I do.

I don't get fatter because I charge around more. I hate sitting still. Garnet will hunch up over a book for hours, but I get the fidgets. We're both quite good at running, Garnet and me. At our last sports day at school we beat everyone, even the boys. We came first. Well, I did, actually. Garnet came second. But that's not surprising, seeing as I'm the eldest. We're both ten. But I'm twenty minutes older. I was the bossy baby who pushed out first. Garnet came second.

We live with our dad and our gran.

Dad often can't tell us apart in the morning at breakfast, but then his eyes aren't always

open properly. He just swallows black coffee
as he shoves on his clothes and then dashes
off for his train. Dad works in an office in
London and he hates it. He's always tired out
when he gets home. But he can tell us apart
by then. It's easier in the evening. My plaits
are generally coming undone and my T-shirt's
probably stained. Garnet stays as neat as a
new pin.

That's what our gran says. Gran always
used to have pins stuck all down the front of
her cardi. We had to be very careful when we
hugged her. Sometimes she even had pins
sticking out of her mouth. That was when she
did her dressmaking. She used to work in this
posh Fashion House, pinning and tucking and
sewing all day long. Then, after . . .

Well, Gran had to look after us, you see, so she did dressmaking at home. For private customers. Mostly very large ladies who wanted posh frocks. Garnet and I always got the giggles when we peeped at them in their underwear.

Gran made all our clothes too. That was *awful*. It was bad enough Gran being old-fashioned and making us have our hair in plaits. But our clothes made us a laughing stock at school, though some of the mums said we looked a picture.

We had frilly frocks in summer and dinky pleated skirts in winter, and Gran knitted too – angora boleros that made us itch, and matching jumpers and cardis for the cold. Twinsets. And a right silly set of twins we looked too.

But then Gran's arthritis got worse. She'd always had funny fingers and a bad hip and a naughty knee. But soon she got so she'd screw up her face when she got up or sat down, and her fingers swelled sideways and she couldn't make them work.

She can't do her dressmaking now. It's a shame, because she did like doing it so much. But there's one Amazing Advantage. We get to wear shop clothes now. And because Gran can't really make it on the bus into town, we get to *choose*.

Well. Ruby gets to choose.

I choose for both of us. T-shirts. Leggings. Jeans. Matching ones, of course. We still want to look alike. We just want to look normal.

Only I suppose we're not really like the normal sort of family you read about in books. We read a lot of books. Dad is the worst. He keeps on and on buying them — not just new ones, but heaps of old dusty tomes from book

fairs and auctions and Oxfam shops. We've
run out of shelves. We've even run out of floor.
We've got piles and piles of books in every
room and you have to zig-zag around them
carefully or you cause a bookquake. If you
have ever been attacked by fifty or a hundred
very hard hardbacks then you'll know this is
to be avoided at all costs. There are big boxes

of books upstairs too that Dad hasn't even
properly sorted. Sometimes you have to climb
right over them to get somewhere vital like
the toilet.

Gran keeps moaning that the floorboards won't stand up to all that weight. They do tend to creak a bit. Dad gets fussed then and agrees it's ridiculous and sometimes when we're a bit strapped for cash he loads a few boxes into our old car and takes them to a second-hand bookshop to sell. He does sell them too – but he nearly always comes back with another lot of bargains, books he couldn't possibly resist.

Then Gran has another fierce nag and Dad goes all shifty, but when he brings her a big carrier of blockbuster romances from a boot fair she softens up considerably. Gran likes to sit in her special chair with lots of plumped-up cushions at her back, her little legs propped up on her pouffe, a box of Cadbury's Milk Tray wedged in beside her, and a juicy love story in her lap. They're sometimes very *rude*, and when Garnet and I read over her shoulder she swats us away, saying we'll find out something we shouldn't. Ho ho. We found it all out *ages* ago.

Dad reads great fat books too, but they're not modern, they're all classics – Charles Dickens and Thomas Hardy. If we have a look at Dad's book we wonder what the Dickens they're on about and they seem *very* Hardy, but Dad likes them. He also likes boys' adventure books – really old ones where the boys wear knickerbockers and talk like twits: 'I say, old bean', and 'Truly spiffing', and 'Tophole'.

Garnet likes old books too – stuff like *Little Women* and *What Katy Did* and all those E. Nesbit books. And she reads twin books too. Books like *The Twins at St Clare's*. And all the *Sweet Valley Twins*. I read them too, because you can read them nice and quickly. But the books *I* like best are true stories about flashy famous people. Actors and actresses. I skip everything boring and just read the best bits when they're on telly and making movies and all over the front of the newspapers, very flashy and very famous.

We're going to be famous too someday, you bet. So I've started writing our life-story already. It's funny, Garnet is usually the one who writes stuff. Her writing's neater than mine. So often I get her to do my schoolwork. She doesn't mind.

Yes I do.

I was rifling through one of the boxes of books upstairs and right at the bottom there was this lovely fat red book. Ruby red, with a leather spine and one word picked out in gold lettering: ACCOUNTS.

I thought it was the title but when I opened it up there were just all these blank pages.

I asked Dad what had happened to the story and he said it wasn't a proper book at all. Accounts are sums. You add up everything you've bought. That's keeping accounts.

'Only I don't like keeping accounts. I just feel guilty seeing how much I've spent,' said Dad. 'You can have it to scribble in, twins.'

So I'm scribbling away.

I'm not.

Yes you are. I keep letting you have a turn. And I'm not just writing about me, I'm writing about us. Giving an account of ourselves. Hey, Garnet, find a dictionary and look up the word 'account'.

Account: 1. A verbal or written report, description, or narration of some occurrence, event, etcetera.

Yeah! That's exactly what I'm doing. Writing an account of our lives.

Everything's a bit boring right this minute but maybe soon we'll somehow get our big chance and we'll achieve our lifetime's ambition and be actresses.

I don't want to be an actress.

Of course we want to be actresses. Honestly, Garnet, give over jogging me. (She can be a bit stupid and shy at times. She doesn't think we'll ever make it as flashy film stars, but I keep telling her all we need is CONFIDENCE. She keeps going on at me now, saying she doesn't want to be a star. Well, that's mad. She can't mean it. Who on earth wouldn't want to show off all day in front of the camera and go to posh parties every night with all the other stars?)
We'll live in our own flash flat with masses

of flowers in every room and huge boxes of chocs to dip into whenever we fancy, and we'll wear ruby-red sequin frocks and ruby jewellery to match – OK OK, Garnet, you can have garnets, only they're not as precious and valuable and sparkly, *are* they?

That's not what you wanted to say? Well, what *do* you want to say then? All right. You write your bit now. Go on. Here you are. Get cracking. You write about you.

I don't know what to put.

I'm not used to writing about me. It's always us. I do like writing though. I was a bit annoyed when Ruby bagged this beautiful red book and started scribbling all that stuff. I thought we could maybe use it to write down our plays. We've always played these pretend games together right from when we were little. We pretend to be other people and make things up. It used to seem so real that it would get muddled into our ordinary life. It can still seem real for me, but Ruby often mucks about and won't play properly. She doesn't like going over and over a play, she just wants me to keep making up new ones for us. She doesn't seem to realize it's hard work. And if we keep starting on new plays then some of the best old plays get forgotten. I want to write them down properly to keep them safe.

I like making up plays and I don't mind acting them out when it's just Ruby and me and we're totally private and imagining it so it could almost be actually happening, but I can't bear proper acting.

Ruby and I were twin sheep in the nativity play when we were still in the Infants and it was one of the most truly awful experiences of my life.

Not the most awful, of course.

That was when

Look, you're not writing any of that sad stuff, I won't let you. This is me again. Ruby. Garnet's just gone off, all humpy because I happened to scratch her a tiny little bit when I snatched the pen. I asked her nicely first. And it's my turn now. You have to be able to take turns fairly when you're twins.

That stuff she wrote is daft anyway. What's the point of writing plays down in books? You should *play* plays. And she's got to be an actress because that's what we've always wanted to be, and while we're still trying to get famous we can do adverts and game shows on the telly. Identical twins are a Mega-Novelty.

Garnet can't reject Fame just because of

that one unfortunate experience being a
sheep when we were little.

She got so worked up and nervous when we
had to perform that she wet herself. On stage.
In front of everyone. But it didn't really
matter. I don't know why she still gets all hot
and bothered if I happen to bring it up. It was
dead appropriate, actually, because that's
what real sheep do all the time. They don't
hang around the stable with their back legs
crossed, holding it in. They go all over the
place. Which is what Garnet did. And
everyone thought it was ever so funny. Except
Garnet.

Got to go now. I can smell Sunday dinner.
Yorkshire pud, yummy yummy yummy in my
tummy.

Ruby! You mean pig. You've put about me being the sheep!

Look, *you* were the one who mentioned it first. You went on and on about it.

Yes, but I didn't say what happened. It was my most painful and humiliating secret. And now you've told, Ruby.

I haven't *told*. I've written. And this accounts book is secret. Just for us. We can write everything down in it. All our secrets.

Yes, but you haven't written down your *secrets. You've written down mine.*

Oh, quit fussing. Let's go and eat. I'm starving.

Gran's a bit cross because Dad's ever so late back from his car-boot sale and she's had the dinner turned down low for the last half-hour and her Yorkshire is going all sad and soggy.

Like some silly twin. Come on, Gran's calling.

Dad should have been back ages ago. He is

all right, isn't he?

Of course he is. You are an old worryguts,
Garnet. He'll have just bought up an entire
bookstall, that's all, and he'll be having
trouble stuffing them all into the car. You
know what he's like.

*Yes, but he's not usually as late as this. And
he likes Gran's Sunday dinners as much as
we do. What if he's had an accident?*

Oh, Garnet, shut up. Coming, Gran.

TWO

We haven't been able to write a proper
account because tons and tons of stuff has
been happening. And now I suppose I should
write it all out and yet I don't know where to
start. You have a go, Garnet. Go on.

*I don't want to go on. I want to stop. No. I
want to go backwards. Back past the day Dad
was late back from the boot fair. Back past the
ordinary us twins and Dad and Granny day
after day part. Back through the awful bit
when Mum died and*

STOP IT STOP IT STOP IT

No, Ruby. We can't stop now. We've got to remember. And don't you see? We've got to make Dad remember. And then he'll stop seeing Rose.

Ah. All right. But tell it quickly. The bit about Mum. Tell it as if it was a story and not real so that it won't hurt so much.

Once upon a time a man called Richard fell in love with a girl called Opal. Opals are beautiful stones that shine all different colours. But some say opals are unlucky. This girl Opal was beautiful and she shone and Richard knew he was lucky lucky lucky to have met her.

Richard loved Opal. He sometimes mucked about and called her Oh Pal. Because he said she was his pal. And he gave her an opal ring.

Where's that ring? Remember how we used to be allowed to try it on? But I haven't seen it for ages. Oh no. Oh Garnet, you don't suppose Dad will give it to *Rose?*

No! Of course not. Gran's got it safe in her jewel box and she says we'll get it when we're grown up.

Which one of us? It ought really to be me, seeing as I'm the eldest. But I'll let you borrow it sometimes. If you're careful.

I'm *the careful one. Look, you've interrupted my story now.*

Go on then. You got to the ring bit. Dad gave Mum the ring.

Richard gave Opal a beautiful opal ring, milky-white but with all different pinks and blues and greens and purples, sparkling like magic whenever it caught the light.

They got their own flat.

They got married.

They had twin daughters.

Which is which? I'm that one, the baby with Mum.

No, that's me. You're the baby with Dad. I drew it so I should know.

Well, I can't help that. The baby with Mum is the biggest baby, you just look and see. And *I* was the biggest, we both know that. That's baby Ruby. I'll show you.

It doesn't matter anyway. OK, you're the baby with Mum.

Right. Well. Mum held you too, of course. She held me and then she held you and Dad held me and then

And then we grew up a bit and we could toddle around and we didn't need to be held. Though we still had cuddles with Mum. We sat on her lap. Both of us together. I can remember.

You're just remembering that photograph. Hey, let's stick it in the accounts book.

It's not just the photo. I can remember. She felt so soft and yet her arms could hold you so

tight you felt safe. And there was her flowery smell, and her curly hair tickled. She tickled us too, remember? Round and round the garden and then she'd tickle us under our arms and we'd go all squirmy. Remember that, Ruby?

(She's gone all quiet. She can't stand remembering because it makes her so sad and she can't ever stand being unhappy. She won't ever cry. That's one of the few ways people tell *us apart. If one of us has gone all red and watery-eyed then it's me.*

I think I might cry a bit when I write this next part. I'll go back to doing it like a story. And I'll scribble it down ever so quickly.)

The twins started school, and Opal and Richard went to work and at the weekend they did fun things like going swimming and shopping and they had days at the seaside. All the normal nice family things. But then everything stopped being normal and nice. Opal got a bit sick. Then she had to go into hospital. She was all right for a bit after that. But then she got sick again. She couldn't work any more. She lay on the sofa at home. Gran had to meet the twins from school. Richard stopped working and looked after Opal. But she couldn't get better. She died. So they stopped being a family.

There. I've written it. Do you want to read what I put, Ruby? No, she doesn't. It was three years ago. When we were seven. But we're ten now and it's all right again. We can't ever be our old family but we're a new family now. Gran lives with us and she's not like a mother, but then no-one can ever be like a mother to us. NO-ONE. NO-ONE AT ALL. ESPECIALLY NOT STUPID FRIZZY DIZZY ROSE.

This is Rose.

No, THIS is Rose.

Yes, that's Rose. Only she's even worse than that. What does Dad see in her? He's the only one that likes her. Gran doesn't like her one little bit.

Gran's face when Dad turned up with Rose that Sunday! We all just stared at her. And Dad came out with all this guff about how she'd helped him when his bag of books broke, and then surprise surprise her car wouldn't start so he'd given her a lift and they'd popped into a pub for a quick drink on the way home and she was all set to have a sandwich for her lunch and Dad said he'd got a proper roast-beef-and-Yorkshire job cooking for him at home and she went Oooh it's ages since I had a proper Sunday dinner like that so guess what, folks. He brought her back. To share our Sunday lunch.

'There's no problem, is there, Gran?' Dad said.

'No, of course not. Do come and sit down at the table, Rose. There's plenty of food. I'm afraid the beef will be a bit overdone and I can't take pride in my Yorkshire today. It *was* lovely and light and fluffy, but . . .'

'But I waylaid your son-in-law and kept him down the pub and mucked up your meal,' said Rose, and she actually laughed. 'Sorry about that,' she said, though she didn't look the *slightest* bit sorry.

Gran had to smile back at her through gritted teeth like it was funny.

We didn't smile though, did we, Garnet?

She couldn't take the hint though. She
chatted away to us, nattering on about telly
programmes and pop records and stuff, as if
she'd known us years and years. And she kept
trying to remember which of us was which.

'Now, you're Garnet, right?' she said to me.
'And you're Ruby,' she said to Garnet.

'Yes,' we said. 'Right.'

'Wrong,' said Dad, laughing uneasily.
'That's Ruby. And that's Garnet. They're a
pair of jokers. Even Gran and I get confused
at times.'

'Speak for yourself,' Gran said huffily. 'I'm
sorry the beef was so dry. Though it would
have been just cooked through a treat an
hour or so ago. Anyway. Apple pie and cream?
Help me clear the plates, girls.'

We helped her clear and when we came

back with the pudding plates I sat in Garnet's chair and she sat in mine. Rose was none the wiser. She nattered away to me, calling me Garnet, and she jabbered stuff to Garnet, calling her Ruby.

'Yes, I'm beginning to be able to tell you apart,' she said. 'You're Ruby. And you're Garnet. Yes. Right.'

'Well. Not *quite* right,' said Dad. He came out with this false ho-ho-ho as if it was a great joke. 'Stop teasing poor Rose, twins. I'm afraid they've swopped seats. They're always doing it. I'd just call each girl "Twin"and be done with it, Rose.'

'Oh, I think that's awful,' said Rose. 'I couldn't stand that if I were a twin.'

Well, certainly twin Roses would be AWFUL.

'You're two separate people who just happen to be sisters, aren't you, Garnet and Ruby. Or Ruby and Garnet. Whichever. I've got muddled.'

'We like being called Twin,' I told her.

'That's what they call us at school,' said Garnet.

'We *are* twins . . .' I said.

'So we like . . .' said Garnet.

'Being called . . .' I said.

'Twins,' we said simultaneously.

33

Rose raised one eyebrow and gave a little nod.

'OK OK,' she said. 'Got it.'

She stopped trying to be so matey with us then. She tried complimenting Gran on her apple pie but Gran stayed as dried up as the dinner and barely said a word. So Dad did all the talking, on and on, saying all this silly stuff and pulling faces and telling stupid stories.

He didn't sound like Dad at all.

It was as if *he'd* swopped with a new twin dad.

He didn't go back to being our dad even when we'd got rid of Rose at last.

'Well, what did you think of her?' he asked eagerly.

I looked at Garnet. She looked at me. I raised one eyebrow. She raised one too. Then we both turned sideways and pretended to be sick.

'All right, all right. You've done enough clowning around for one day,' Dad said crossly.

'Yes, don't be so rude, Ruby and Garnet,' said Gran – but she didn't sound a bit cross.

'Did you like Rose, Gran?' Dad asked.

'Well. She seems nice enough. I suppose. A bit . . . pushy, inviting herself to lunch like that.'

'No, I invited her,' said Dad. 'I didn't think you'd make such a big deal about it, actually. You've always said you wished I'd socialize a bit more, bring a few friends home, not stay so wrapped up in the past.'

'Yes, dear. And I mean that. I'm only too pleased that you want to bring people back. Though if you could have just phoned to give me a bit of warning . . . And you do want to go a bit carefully with that type of woman.'

'What do you mean, *type*?' said Dad, really angry now.

'Now, Richard, don't get in such a silly state,' said Gran, as if he was our age. 'It's just that she seems a bit eager. She's never set eyes on you before today and yet she's all over you, even trying to act like one of the family.'

'I've known Rose for months, if you must know,' said Dad. 'She's got her own bric-a-brac stall in the arcade – we're forever bumping into each other at boot fairs. I've always wanted to get to know her better, she's so bubbly and warm and friendly. I don't know how you can talk about her like that – she's a lovely girl.'

'Girl!' said Gran. 'She'll never see thirty again.'

'Well, neither will I,' Dad shouted. 'And it's about time I started making the most of my life, OK?'

He stormed off out of the house, slamming the door. There was a horrible silence after he'd left. Garnet got hold of my hand and squeezed it tight. She looked like she was going to cry. *Gran* looked like she was going to cry too.

We were all shocked by the row. We don't ever have rows in our family.

It's all that Rose's fault.

Yes, it's all Rose's fault. She started all the changes. She comes every Sunday now. And in the week sometimes. And Dad goes out with her in the evenings and when they come back in the car, they KISS.

THREE

*I hate changes. I want every day to be the
same. I've always been like it, even before
Mum died.*

I couldn't stand our first day at school.

*Everybody stared at us because we were
different. And the whole day was different. We
couldn't play our own games and talk in our*

own private language. It felt like we couldn't even be twins, because the teacher sat me on one side of the classroom and Ruby on the other. She said it was so she could tell us apart.

I felt as if she'd somehow torn us apart. I didn't feel a whole person at all. I felt like a half, as if an arm and a leg and most of my head were the other side of the room stuck to Ruby. I didn't know how to think without her.

Well, naturally. I'm the oldest. I'm the DOMINANT twin. That's what they call the one that's born first. That's me. I'm the Big Cheese. You're just the Little Crumb.

You didn't like us being separated either, Ruby. You didn't cry

You did.

but you were ever so naughty and so we got
sent to the headteacher and she said, 'Why are
you so unhappy, Garnet? Why are you so
naughty, Ruby?' and we said, 'We want to sit
together.' And she said, 'Is that all? Simple!'

And it was simple. We sat together. I didn't
cry any more. And Ruby wasn't naughty. Well,
she was, but not so much.

But it still took me ages and ages to get
used to school. But now it's OK. Everyone's so
used to us they don't stare. We're just The
Twins. That's the way we want it. We sit
together in every lesson. We're always
partners. We sit next to each other at lunch.
We even go to the loo together.

We're good at lessons. We sometimes come
top, especially when we have to write stories or
do a project.

But we like Drama best. We're absolutely fabulous at Drama. Well. *I* am. Garnet goes all red and gets her words mixed up.

Don't start, Ruby.

Well, you do. Only you wouldn't if you'd stop being so shy. I don't know why you're so shy. *I* never feel shy.

Look, I just want to write about

You've been writing for ages and ages and you keep waffling on about us back in the Infants and who's bothered about baby stuff like that? Write about what's happening now. All the horrible bit.

Well, give me the pen.

Say please then. Hey! Get off!
'Are you two girls having a fight?'
That's Gran. She's seen us snatching the pen from each other.
'You can share nicely if you try. Now you're going to have to remember all I've taught you when you go. *She's* not the type to bother with good manners.'
'Oh, Gran. I don't want to go!' I said, and I

flung myself on to her lap.

'Watch my hip! And my knee! Ruby, you great lump, get off of me,' said Gran – but she cuddled me close all the same.

'Can I come and join in the cuddle too?' I asked.

I sat on the arm of the chair so I didn't hurt Gran's other hip and knee, but she reached out and pulled me properly on to her lap.

We clung tight. I started crying.

'Stop it, Garnet,' said Ruby, and she pinched me hard. Her face was all screwed up. She was scared I'd make her start crying, even though she never cries. Gran's eyes were all watery too.

'Dear oh dear,' she said, sniffling. She patted us with her poor hands, the fingers all slipping sideways with arthritis. She fumbled up the sleeve of her cardi for her hankie and mopped my face and hers, and then pretended to blow Ruby's nose.

'We'd better turn off the waterworks. I don't want a puddle in my chair,' said Gran.

'Oh Gran, please please please come with us,' Ruby begged.

'Now don't you start, young Ruby. You know it's all settled and decided.'

'But we'll miss you so, Gran!' I said, nuzzling into her warm woollen chest.

'And I'll miss both of you, my girls. But you can come and stay with me on visits – you can sleep either end of the sofa and bring your sleeping bags – and I'll maybe come to this new place for Christmas.'

'Not maybe. You've GOT to come.'

'We'll see. Of course, there's probably no point. She doesn't have a clue about cooking. She probably won't even bother to have a proper turkey.'

'So why can't we all come to you for Christmas, Gran, and then we can have Christmas dinner the way you do it, with cranberry sauce and little chipolatas and chestnut stuffing, yummy yummy,' said Ruby.

'That oven in my new flat is so small it would be hard put to cook a chicken in it,' said Gran. 'Sorry, pet. No more Christmas dinners.'

'No more roast potatoes with special crispy bits and Christmas pud with little silver charms and traffic-light jelly, red and yellow and green,' Ruby wailed.

'I think you're going to miss my cooking more than you'll miss me,' said Gran, shaking her head. 'Come on now, you're both squashing me something chronic. You'd better get back to your writing. Is it something for school?'

There's no point doing anything for school. Because we won't be going there much longer. We've got to go to a new school. In a new place. In a new life. And we're going to hate it.

It's all her fault. We hate her. WE HATE HER.

*Yes. We hate her. It all started when Dad
met Rose. She kept coming round upsetting
us. Barging in. Changing things.*

She changed Dad. It isn't just the way he
acts, all loopy and lovey-dovey, yuck yuck
yuck. She's changed his clothes. He always
used to wear just ordinary Dad clothes.
Jumpers. Trousers. Suits and white shirts on
weekdays, with stripy ties. She started with
the ties. She bought him this bright red
flowery number.

Then it was Marilyn Monroe. And Mickey
Mouse. Dad looked a bit of a cartoon himself
in all these daft ties. She didn't stop there.
Oh no.

Would you believe, Donald Duck
underpants!

At least they were hidden under his
trousers. She started on his shirts next.
Green stripes. Red check. Blue polka dot.

She said they brightened up his dull old
suit.

She was worse with his weekend clothes.
She made him give his tracksuit and his
comfy old cords to Oxfam. She said they were
old man's clothes. She's turned Dad into a
new man. A new stupid trendy twit of a dad

in black jeans and
denim jackets and
lumberjack shirts.

She even calls him a new name. Rick. It's
Rick this, Rick that. Sometimes it's even
Ricky. It doesn't half make you feel Sicky.

Gran can't bear it either.

'His name's *Richard*,' she hissed one day.
'We've always called him Richard. No-one
ever calls him Ricky or Rick.'

She said it in the sort of voice that makes
Garnet squirm. But Rose isn't the squirmy
sort. She just smiled.

'*I* call him Rick,' she said.

Gran scowled and sucked her teeth.

'Oh dear,' said Rose sympathetically. 'Is the
pain really bad today?'

Rose is the Pain.

But Gran is in pain too. Her arthritis has got horrid. Sometimes she can't even get out of bed and Ruby and I have to help her. And it takes her ages and ages to get down the stairs with her hip. And up the stairs to the loo. And when she's in her chair she gets stuck and we have to heave, Ruby one side, me the other.

How is she going to manage without us helping her?

She's moving to sheltered housing. We thought that meant she was being housed in a bus shelter.

It's not as bad as that. It's a little flat on the ground floor and she's going to have a Home Help and an Alarm Button.

I feel as if I have an Alarm Button inside me and it's going off all the time.

We're moving too. Garnet and me. And
Dad. And *Her*. Dad lost his job. It's called
Being Made Redundant. Dad said he didn't
care. He'd always hated that boring old office.
But he looked a bit shocked all the same.

'So how are you going to manage without
your boring old salary?' said Gran, sniffing.
'Oh, Richard, you're such a fool. How could
you spoil all your chances like this? And
you've got the twins to think of, too.'

'It wasn't my fault,' he said.

'You've never shown the right attitude. And
since you've taken up with that Rose, you've
turned into . . . into a *hippy*.'

'Oh, for goodness sake—'

'Those silly ties and shirts were the last
straw. Of course they got rid of you. So what
are you going to do now? Have you looked at
the Jobs Vacant in the papers?'

'I don't want that sort of job any more,' said
Dad. 'I've been thinking. They're giving me
quite a bit of cash as my redundancy pay. It's
my chance for a whole new start. We could
sell up here, get a little shop in the country
somewhere. A bookshop. You've always been
on and on at me to sell some of my books!'

'You're talking nonsense,' said Gran. 'Well,
count me out.'

Count us out too, Dad! Garnet and me. We

don't want to be part of any of this.

We don't want to move to a silly old shop in the country! We don't want to leave Gran. We don't want to leave all our friends. We don't want to leave our school. We don't want to leave our old lives. We don't want to live with you. Not if it means we've got to live with *her*. Because she's coming too. Rose.

We wish she'd get greenfly and mildew and wilt.

FOUR

If our writing's a bit shaky, it's because we're
doing this account in the van.

We feel shaky. Our whole lives have been
shaken up.

Dad really has bought a bookshop! He
didn't even take us with him to check it out
first. He went away for the weekend with
Rose, and when he came back he said, 'Guess
what! I've bought a shop.'

We just stared at him, stunned. He's been
acting so crazy. Not like a dad at all.
Especially not our dad.

We're used to him saying, 'Guess what! I've
bought another box of books.'

But you don't buy a book*shop* just like that.
You're meant to hang around for months,
getting it surveyed and seeing solicitors.

'It's all simple,' said Dad. 'This sweet old
couple are retiring and are happy to move out
straightaway. If I can't sell our own house, I'll
let it out to students for a bit. Your gran's got
her sheltered flat all worked out. Rose only
rents her room, and she can shut up her stall
in the arcade any time, so she hasn't got any
problems either.'

We're the ones with the problems. Garnet
and me.

We don't even get considered.

'Why didn't you take us with you to see if
we like it?' I said.

'You'll love it,' said Dad. 'The village is right
out in the country, beside a river, with hills
all around. It's a real story-book place.
There's a pond with puddleducks straight out
of Beatrix Potter. There's just this one street
of shops. Ours is in the middle. We'll fit it out
with shelves and Rose can have the window
for her bric-a-brac. She's got all sorts of ideas

for getting it done up. And there's plenty of room upstairs. You two can have the attic for your bedroom – you'll like that.'

Sarah Crewe gets stuck in an attic in A Little Princess *and she has to act like a servant to all the girls in her school. Though at least she got to* stay *in her school.*

We've had to leave our school.
It was awful saying goodbye.

But it was much worse saying goodbye to

Ruby doesn't want to write it. She always leaves the worst bit to me. I don't want to write it either.

*Oh, Gran. We do miss you. We miss you ever
so ever so much. You used to get cross and you
were strict and sometimes you even smacked,
but you didn't hurt because of your poor
hands and you couldn't help being strict
because you're old and you were only cross
when we were naughty.*

*But we do so wish you were with us now.
You could be cross and strict and smack all
the time and we wouldn't mind a bit.*

*You didn't get cross and strict and smack
when we took you to your new flat. But you
weren't all happy and smiley. You looked so
small and scrunched up and sad and it was
so awful.*

*We helped you put your chair and your
china cabinet and all the rest of your stuff in
your new room, but they didn't look right.
They didn't look yours. It didn't look like a
home.*

*This funny old man next door came round
to say hello and he gave you a bunch of
flowers he'd grown in his garden. Dad teased
you and said you'd got yourself a boyfriend
already, but you wouldn't smile. And when
Dad said he hoped you'd be really happy in
your new flat and he was sure it was all for
the best, you just sniffed. You didn't say
anything, but you looked at Dad and it was as*

if you were shrieking: Who are you kidding?

You didn't even kiss Dad properly goodbye, just gave him your cheek. And we don't blame you either, Gran.

You kissed us. And we kissed you. Lots and lots.

We didn't talk to Dad either. We're still not speaking to him properly. Or Rose. We don't need to. We can just speak to each other. In Twinspeak, so they can't understand.

Garnet and I have this special language. We've got heaps of made-up words for things. Sometimes we don't use words at all, we use signs. Little tiny things like widening our eyes or putting our heads slightly to one side. We signal to each other and then both start up a pretend coughing fit or sneeze simultaneously or shriek with manic laughter.

Rose isn't used to this. It doesn't half make her jump.

'Pack it in,' says Dad.

I glance at Garnet.

'Pack it in what, Dad?' we say simultaneously.

'Less of the cheek,' says Dad, taking one hand off the steering wheel and swatting at us.

'How do they *do* that?' Rose asks.

'How do we do what?' we say.

'Stop it! You're giving me the creeps. Can you really read each other's thoughts?' she says, shivering.

'Of course they can't,' says Dad.

'Then how can they say the same thing at the same time in that weird way?' Rose says, peering at us.

'I don't know,' says Dad, shrugging.

'*We* know,' we say, and we raise our eyebrows and make our eyes glitter in a mysterious and mystic manner.

We wait until Rose turns round again and starts fiddling with the old van radio, trying to tune it to a station. I point to it and nudge Garnet. We both start singing loudly, our timing spot on.

Rose gasps.

'Cut it out, twins,' says Dad sharply.

I turn my fingers into pretend scissors and

make lots of cutting movements. Garnet does the same.

'Oh, very funny,' says Dad, not at all amused.

When he's concentrating on the road, I change the scissors to a dagger and mime a sudden bloody attack on Rose. Garnet does likewise, only she's not quite quick enough. Dad sees, so Garnet shakes her arm quickly, making out she's got cramp.

'What are you playing at, you two?' says Dad.

We blink at him and shrug.

Dad sighs with exasperation, and then takes one hand off the steering wheel and puts his arm round Rose.

I nudge Garnet and we both make a very rude noise.

Dad's hand tightens on Rose's shoulder, but he doesn't say anything. She doesn't say anything either. Neither do we. The radio keeps buzzing and fading and going funny.

I feel a bit like that too. Maybe I'm starting to feel car-sick. Well, van-sick. Ooh good, if I'm going to throw up then I shall aim at Rose.

Ruby was sick. She managed to hit Rose. And me.

Only little splashes on you.

You're not supposed to be writing, in case you get sick again.

I did great, didn't I?

Yes, but I'd sooner you didn't do it again. Rose got through a whole box of tissues, mopping away. Dad had to stop at the next service station and we had to go to the Ladies. I washed and Ruby washed. Rose positively scrubbed and changed her sweater and jeans, scrunching the stained smelly stuff into a plastic bag.
'I think you two belong in the bag too,' she said, sighing. 'Look, I don't care if you act like idiots, but it isn't half upsetting your dad.'

We didn't say anything. But Ruby smiled, even though she was still sick and shivery.

'Don't you want your dad to be happy?' said Rose, looking at Ruby and then at me.

Not with you!

'He's had a really tough time the last few years. You two were only tiny so you probably didn't realize, but he nearly went to pieces after your mum died.'

We stared at her silently, hating her. How dare she! We felt like we were in little pieces too.

'It was really tough for him, but he kept on going for your sake. He did his best to get on with your gran, even though she can be so difficult at times.'

How does she have the nerve to criticize our gran!

'He didn't have any fun, he never went out anywhere, he was so lonely,' she said.

How could he possibly have been lonely? He had us!

'He kept slaving away at that boring old job in the city, even though it nearly drove him crazy. He was like this old old man even though he's barely thirty.'

She's mad. He's our dad. He is old.

'But now he's got this big chance. A whole new life. Something that he's always wanted.

*And he's been like a little kid – so excited. But
you two are spoiling it all. Can't you see that?'*

*Yes, we can see it. That's what we want. It's
not us that's spoiling anything. She's got it all
wrong. It's her. It's her it's her it's her.*

FIVE

We're here. And we hate it.

Yes. We hate it.

It's the worst place in the whole world, and we're stuck here with the worst people. Stuck stuck stuck.

Well, the place itself isn't that bad.

Yes it is!

No, wait, Ruby. I don't mean the shop. Or the village. But the countryside itself is OK, isn't it? Especially the hills. I hated going for a walk with Rose and Dad, but when we were up in the hills and we saw all the sheep and the wild ponies and we got right to the top and we were almost up in the sky and we could see for miles and it felt like we could just step off the edge and fly—

Will you put a sock in it, Miss Arty-Farty Show-Off. All this sky-and-fly stuff! You sound like you're writing a poem for school. 'My-day-in-the-country'. Boring! And the country's boring too. Grey hills and grey fields and grey trees and grey rain.

Rose doesn't think much of it either. She's still all smarmy with Dad, but we're wearing her down – and this certainly isn't her dream place to live. She got seriously fed up when I accidentally on purpose waved that branch near the washing line and snagged all her stupid tights and the village shop only sells

pale beige old-lady tights. Old Rose could have sold her soul for a Sock Shop then.

She hates the Superstore too. Because it doesn't have any decent fruit or veg and the bread's sliced up in bags.

Yes, but Dad says he'll grow raspberries and tomatoes and runner beans in the back garden and he's going to have a go at making our own bread.

Do me a favour, Garnet! Dad can't even make *toast*. Gran was always going on about how hopeless he was.

Dad says that was because she never let him try his hand at anything. She always said, 'Come on now, out from under my feet, stop cluttering up my kitchen.' Oh dear. We do miss Gran so. We wish she was here.

No, we wish *we* were *there*. Instead of here in this hateful dump. We don't fit in.

Dad's shop doesn't fit in either. Especially now. The antique shops are all painted white or cream or very pale beige. Dad's shop started off dirty white too, so he decided to brighten it up a bit.

'I'm going to call it The Red Bookshop,' he

said. 'Because of my three girls. Rubies are
red, Garnets are red, and Roses are red. So
let's go the whole hog and paint it red too.'

He motored miles and miles to the nearest
Do-it-Yourself Store in Hineford and came
back with pots of stinging scarlet paint. We
were supposed to help Rose wash the front of
the shop and rub the peeling paint, but after
about ten minutes scrubbing and sloshing,
Ruby threw her sponge in the bucket and said,
'We're fed up with this lark,' and sauntered
off.

So I threw my sponge in the bucket too, and
sidled after my sister.

'Hey, come back, you lazy beasts,' Rose
shouted, and she threw a sponge at us.

It glanced off Ruby, still sopping wet. Ruby
took hold of it and aimed. She's a very good
aimer. It caught Rose full in the face.

We ran right away then. We walked round and round the village and up and down the stream and then we went down by the river but it was too muddy and we weren't wearing our wellies and I slipped and got mud all over my bottom. It looked AWFUL. And Ruby made it worse because she kept laughing at me. I tried to rub the mud off with grass but it was useless.

I started to cry and Ruby got cross.

'Why do you always have to be such a baby?' she said. 'Look, it's your own fault for slipping like that. And it doesn't matter anyway – they're only your old jeans. And she can't tell us off because she's not our mother or any part of our family. So stop snivelling.'

'I can't go back through the village like this. People will look at me and laugh.'

'No they won't. They won't even notice, honest,' said Ruby.

She wasn't being honest. They did notice. This crowd of children fishing by the bridge saw us and stared. First of all because we were strangers. Second because we're twins. But then they saw the muck all over my jeans and then they really stared. And sniggered. And shouted horrible rude suggestions.

Ruby caught hold of me by the wrist and gave me a little shake to stop me crying again.

She marched us straight up to them instead of
skulking away, like I wanted. Her face was as
red as her name.

'What's so funny?' she said, when we were
right up close to them. She made me say it too.
'What's so funny?' we said in unison.

They were mostly around our age, but some
were bigger. Ruby didn't care.

Some of the littler kids stepped backwards.
They weren't just worried about Ruby. It was
me too. Because we were walking in step and
talking exactly together and when we do that
lots of people find it really spooky.

The bigger boys weren't easily fazed though.
One fat one with silly sideways hair said
something ever so rude and horrible and they
all laughed again.

'Ooh! Being covered in mud is funny, is it?'
said Ruby.

'Funny, is it?' we said together.

Then Ruby looked at me and looked at the muddy grass and I knew what she was going to do. I knew I had to do it too. We bent, we sunk our hands into the mud, we straightened up – and while they were still all gawking at us we went splat, right in their faces.

'Have a big laugh then,' said Ruby – and we ran.

They started running after us, but we can be very speedy so we soon got clean away. Well. I wasn't clean. I was still covered in mud.

· 'But so are they!' Ruby spluttered breathlessly. 'Their faces. Oh, Garnet, that was so glorious. Twin-grin!'

'Twin-grin,' I echoed obediently, though I didn't really feel like smiling.

We have this little grinning ritual whenever we're really pleased about something. Ruby puts her fingers at the corners of my mouth and turns it into a huge grin, while I reach out at the same time and do the same to her.

I managed to stay grinning like a Halloween pumpkin, but I kept looking behind me all the same, in case those children might be creeping up on us.

'Relax. They'll have gone back to their stupid fishing,' said Ruby, sussing that I was still scared.

'Maybe. But they'll still be out to get us sometime, won't they,' I said stiffly, trying to keep my grin in place.

'Well, we'll get them back,' said Ruby airily. 'Especially that Big Blobby one.'

'But they'll all start hating us then. And we've got to go to school with them, haven't we,' I said. My grin wavered, and then drooped.

'We won't go to this dumb old school. We'll slope off by ourselves,' said Ruby.

'But they'll find out and we'll get into trouble,' I said. 'And we're in pretty big trouble now. We can't go home because Rose will get us, and we can't go down by the river because those children will get us.'

It looked like we were stuck for ever, hiding up a little alleyway at the edge of the village. I leant against the wall, the cold pebbly stuff scratching me through my T-shirt. My jeans were still wet and sticky with mud. My face ached with trying to smile. My eyes stung with trying not to cry again.

'Garnet?' said Ruby gently.

She put her arm round me and cuddled me close. I snuggled up against her and we held on tight to each other. Our shadows became Siamese.

'Perhaps we'd better go back to the bookshop,' I said eventually.

'No, not yet. We've only been gone an hour or so. She'll just get angry. No, we have to stay away ages and ages, and then she'll be really worried. Better to stay away until after Dad gets back, then he'll be dead worried too, and they'll maybe have a go at each other. Then when we do turn up they'll be so relieved we've not been kidnapped or killed that they won't go on at us. Or not so much, anyway.'

'But what are we going to do?' I wailed.

'We'll do one of our plays,' said Ruby.
That made me cheer up. Ruby hasn't felt
like playing one of our pretend games for ages.
So we had this really great game together.

And then, when we eventually sloped back
to the shop, Rose didn't get cross with us.
She'd done all the front of the shop by
herself, but she didn't tell on us to Dad. She
even washed out my jeans for me without
getting fussed. Gran would have gone nuts.

What's the matter with you, Garnet? Have
you **gone completely nuts? Is this Let's Love**
Rosy-Posy Day?

No. I can't stick her, you know that. But I'm
just trying to write a truthful account, that's
all. In our accounts book.

Well, I think we should give a good account of ourselves. And make a bad account of everyone else. That's much more fun.

Rose was OK when that woman in the quilty jacket and the lollopy dog came to complain about the red paint.

Dad looked like he was going to burst into tears, but Rose went 'Oh B-B-B-R-R-R-R-R-R-R-R-R!', blowing this giant raspberry and said it was our shop and we could paint it whatever colour we fancied and that the video shop two doors along with all its placards didn't exactly add to the authentic Victorian charm of the village anyway. So the bossy lady got into a huff and flounced out with her floppy dog and we were all laughing—

Yes, but Rose wasn't really that clever, because how many real customers has Dad had?

Well, there was the man who wanted the gardening book . . . and the lady who wanted all the Bills and Moons . . . lots of ladies . . .

Yes, but they only spend fifty pence at a time!

That vicar came. And he bought a Bible – the big one with pictures that cost heaps.

And that's about *it*. They don't want to come, the villagers. They don't like us. Or they don't like books. Or both.

Yes, but Dad says he's really after the Tourist Trade. The people who come at weekends. And holidaymakers.

Who'd ever want to come and have a
holiday in this old dump? All right, the shop
did get quite busy last Saturday and Sunday,
but hardly anybody *bought* anything.
There were the hikers

and they left mud all over the place.
There were the bikers

and they dripped ice-cream everywhere. And there was that family who asked to use the toilet.

None of that lot bought a sausage.

One of the bikers bought an old Beano *annual.*

Oh, big deal. I'm telling you, Garnet. Dad's going to go bust in six months.

Come on, let's play. Make the most of our free time. Because we're starting at our new school on Monday, yuck yuck yuck.

SIX

It's awful. We knew it would be. It's like a
little toy school. There's hardly any
playground. There aren't any computers.
There isn't even a television. The teacher
writes stuff up on a blackboard and we sit at
these dinky little desks with lids and
inkwells. It's like the sort of classroom you
get in a cartoon.

Miss Debenham isn't a bit like that, Ruby!
This is Miss Debenham.

Yes, and she made me feel positively sick and squirmy inside when she stood us in front of the class and introduced us – and as if we *needed* introducing anyway. We're famous in this dreary dump of a village. Everyone knows us.

Especially Jeremy Treadgold and his gang.

Fancy that great Blob being in our class. It's a wonder he can cram himself into the teeny-weeny desk. Imagine having to sit next to him.

I'm glad we can sit together, anyway. Miss Debenham asked us what we'd prefer. Teachers don't usually ask you stuff like that,

they just tell you what they want you to do.
And I like some of the lessons, like when we
had to write about twins.

You can be a real smarmy little creep at
times! I had it all sussed out.

THE GOOD THINGS ABOUT BEING A TWIN

Everything

THE BAD THINGS ABOUT BEING A TWIN

Nothing

And then you were supposed to do your
mirror-writing trick. It would have been so
brilliant:

THE GOOD THINGS ABOUT BEING A TWIN

Everything

THE BAD THINGS ABOUT BEING A TWIN

Nothing

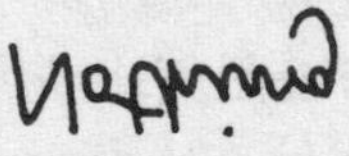

It would have been PERFECT. An answer, and a twin answer. Identical, like us.

But oh no, Miss Suck-up-to-the-teacher-smarty-farty has to write all that rubbish.

THE GOOD THINGS ABOUT BEING A TWIN

There are lots and lots of good things about being a twin. You're never alone, you've always got a best friend to talk to and play with. You can have all sorts of special secrets and make up wonderful games that no-one else can ever understand. You can say things together and do things together so that you can have twice the power.

THE BAD THINGS ABOUT BEING A TWIN

There aren't many bad things about being a twin. Just occasionally it might be peaceful to be alone. Not to have to talk or make up games or listen to secrets. Just to be yourself. Not part of anyone else. You.

Very *bad*, Garnet! Do you *really* want to be left alone? OK, I'll run off the next time that Big Blob tries to get us.

Oh, that was so awful! He crept up on us with this huge great wiggly worm in either hand, and I can't stand worms.

Well, I'm not absolutely enchanted with them myself. Especially not squirming down my jumper. But I got mine out. I shoved it straight down the Big Blob's trousers!

Judy said he once put a worm down her neck too. Judy just about went bananas. She said—

I'm not the slightest bit interested in Judy and what she said. I don't know why you wanted to go off with her.

She's quite nice, Ruby, really she is. And I didn't go off with her, you know that. Miss Debenham said she wanted us to do this big Noah's Ark painting to brighten up the classroom wall and she was going round the whole form asking them which animal they wanted to paint, and I kept hoping nobody else would bag a giraffe, because they're our favourite animal, so when she got to us I said, 'Giraffe' quick. And Miss Debenham smiled at you too and said, 'And you'll do a twin giraffe, right, Ruby?'

So I said, 'Wrong, Miss Debenham. I don't want to paint any stupid old giraffe.'

But why did you say that? And why did you have to choose a flea for your animal?

Simple. One little blob. Flea finished. And if you'd only shut up and waited for *me* to answer old Dumbo Debenham, you could have done a flea too. Then we could have just sat and mucked around for the rest of the lesson. But oh no, you have to go off with that ghastly Judy girl and paint stupid giraffes with her.

I didn't go off – well, not deliberately. I couldn't help it that Judy said she wanted to do a giraffe too. And I tried to back out, you know I did. But Miss Debenham said, 'No, come on, Garnet, you said you'd like to do a giraffe. So you can do the giraffes with Judy. Never mind what Ruby wants to do.'

79

Yes, never mind *me*.

Oh, Ruby. Don't be like that.

I'll be exactly how I want. If you want to pal around with Judy then fine, you go off with her.

I don't want to pal around with her.

So why did you let her tag around with us at playtime then? Going gab gab gab until I felt like punching her in the gob.

Well, what could I do? I couldn't tell her to go away.

I could.

You did. You were ever so rude to her. And I keep telling you, Ruby, she's good fun, she really is — you'd like her if you could bother to get to know her.

I'm not going to get to know any of them. OK. You go and have good fun with your super new friend. Pal around with her all you like. Just don't expect to pal around with *me*.

Ruby! Don't let's quarrel. I hate it so. Ruby, come back. Please.

SEVEN

Ruby?

I can't STAND it when Ruby won't talk to me. It's as if most of me goes missing. As if my own mouth won't work, my own hands won't hold.

She's right. I was crazy to write that stuff about being a twin. It's awful being on your own.

Ruby wouldn't talk to me all yesterday evening. When I tried saying anything she put her hands over her ears and went Bla-bla-bla so she couldn't hear.

After we'd had tea, Ruby went up to our room and started reading an old Beano annual. I said I was sorry, but she didn't look up. I tried putting my arm round her but she wriggled away. I took hold of the Beano annual to make her look at me but she grabbed it back and hit me on the head with it. It hurt quite a lot, but that wasn't really why I was crying.

Ruby didn't take any notice at all.

My nose started to run so badly that I had to go and get a tissue. Rose saw me before I could mop myself up.

'Oh, sweetie,' she said, and she pulled one of her chiffony scarves off her neck and wiped my nose with it. 'Hey, I'm just popping down to that video shop because there's nothing good on telly tonight. Come and help me choose a good film, eh?'

I didn't know what to do. I knew Ruby would never forgive me if I palled up with Rose. But it didn't look like she would ever forgive me anyway.

'Come on, we'll get some chocs too,' said Rose. She rubbed her tummy. 'I've put on a good half-stone since we got here. Still, never mind, eh?'

I wanted to go with Rose. Ruby might not even know unless she looked out of our window. No, who was I kidding? It's like Ruby can look through a little window straight into my head.

'I'd better not,' I mumbled to Rose. 'I mean, I don't feel like it.'

'You don't always have to do what Ruby wants,' Rose said.

She can tell us apart now. Unless we deliberately trick her. She thinks she's getting to know us. But she can't ever really understand. I don't always get it myself. But I do have to do what Ruby wants. Because if I don't, this happens. And it's so horrid.

Rose usually chooses love films with big hunky men, but this time she brought back The Railway Children. *It's one of my all-time favourite films, but generally when we watch it Ruby mucks around and mocks all the accents and at the end when Bobbie runs to*

her father at the station and it's so lovely,
Ruby makes sick noises and switches it off
before it's finished.

Dad raised his eyebrows a bit when he saw
which film it was, but he didn't say anything.
He usually sits on the sofa with Rose, but this
evening he sat in the armchair and he caught
hold of me and sat me on his lap while Rose
put her feet up on the sofa, a box of Cadbury's
Dairy Milk balanced on her tummy. She kept
throwing Dad and me chocolates. I said I
wasn't very hungry thanks, but Dad popped
my favourite chocolate fudge into my mouth
as I spoke and I couldn't really spit it out.

They were being so nice to me, but it didn't
work. The chocolate didn't have any taste. The
Railway Children got started but I couldn't
watch it properly. I kept glancing up at the
ceiling, at Ruby crouched up above us all on
her own.

'Why don't we ask if she feels like coming
down now?' Rose said.

Dad and I looked at each other. Rose certainly doesn't understand Ruby yet.

Rose went up all the same. She left a couple of chocolates beside Ruby. They weren't touched when I came to bed.

Ruby and I always share the bathroom and do synchronized tooth-cleaning, but Ruby barged straight past me and banged the door in my face. When we got into our nighties in the bedroom she seemed to be staring straight through me, as if I didn't exist. That was exactly the way I felt.

When we were in bed with the light off I kept whispering to her, but she wouldn't answer. I lay awake for ages and ages and ages. In the middle of the night I slipped out of my bed and climbed in beside Ruby. She was snoring softly, deep in a dream, but she still wouldn't cuddle up

and after a while I crept back to my own bed.

I think I slept a bit but now I'm wide awake again, even though it's not properly morning.

I think Ruby's awake too.

Ruby?

She's still not speaking.

But I know what to do now.

I did it. And we're friends again now, aren't we, Ruby?

Yeah. OK, OK. Get *off* of me, Garnet!

Make friends, make friends, never never break friends?

I said, didn't I?

Write it too. Write it down here, in the accounts book. Write that you'll never break friends with me again.

I will never break friends with my twin sister and best friend Garnet Barker.

Oh, you've really written it! And put: I swear.

I swear my twin sister and best friend Garnet Barker is driving me completely batty with all this sloppy junk, and if she doesn't shut up soon I might well go back on my promise.

You can't do that. No backsies.

I was only teasing, stupid. Here, what's all this drivel you've been writing? Whimpering on about me for page after page?

Don't look at it now. You're right. It was just rubbish.

So you had chocolate fudge downstairs, did you?

I didn't mean to – I just had my mouth open and—

Oh, well. I might as well eat up my choccies too. One . . . Yum yum yum.

And two . . . Gobble, gobble, gobble. Don't look at me like that. You had yours last night.

Only one.

Well look, here . . .

It's all chewed and slobbery!

Well, we're twins, aren't we? Your slobber is the same as my slobber. My drool is the same as your drool. My spit is the same as your spit.

Your spit is a lot splashier than mine.

Hey, wasn't it great today when we got Jeremy Blob splat-splat! Oh boy oh boy! That was the most terrific supersonic idea of mine, eh? Going up to him in the playground and saying stuff ever so ever so softly so he shakes his head and screws up his face. 'What?' he says. 'I can't hear you?'

So we go, 'Then wash your ears out' and you spit . . . SPLAT. And *I* spit . . . SPLAT. In his ears.

I wish Miss Debenham hadn't been walking across the playground though. She wasn't very pleased either when I said I didn't want to

finish my giraffe and I did a twin flea to match yours. And Judy was a bit fed up too, because now she's lumbered doing one and three-quarters giraffes by herself.

Still, we don't care, do we?

It doesn't matter, so long as we've got each other.

So now school's a doddle, because Garnet and I don't do anything. We just sit looking blank when Dumbo Debenham gets on to us. Or I write the barest minimum and Garnet does mirror-writing. Or we copy everything twice – two lots of sums, two maps, two fact-sheets, because we say everything's got to be doubled because we're a double ourselves.

'Double trouble,' said Dumbo Debenham, and she sighed and tried separating us, Garnet right at the back of the class and me at the front.

It didn't work. Garnet just had to keep her eye on me. I'd tilt my head one way, and that was the signal to sneeze simultaneously. Or I'd tilt my head the other way and we'd both tip our books off the desk. Or I'd nod very slightly and we'd both stand up and say in unison, 'Please may I go to the toilet, Miss

Debenham?' and then we'd walk out keeping step, me first, Garnet second, left right, left right, our arms swinging right left, right left, and then when I gave the slightest little cough we'd toss our heads so that our plaits would go left right, left right, over our shoulders.

And all the kids would stare with their mouths open.

We even spook Jeremy Blob!

But it looks like we're in double trouble with Dad. Dumbo Debenham phoned him up and told tales on us!

'So why are you acting so stupidly at school?' Dad demanded.

'I think they act stupidly at home too!' said Rose.

'We only act–'

'Stupid—'

'To stupid—'

'People,' we said.

But then Dad shook us. Hard. I thought he might even bang our heads together.

'Stop it! I won't have you talking to Rose like that. What's the matter with you? I just don't get it. You've always been such good girls. Well, you've had your moments, Ruby, but you've never ever behaved as badly as this before. And you've both always done so well at school. I've been so proud of you. But now it sounds as if you're going out of your way to be as naughty and disruptive as possible. And you're not even trying to make friends with the other children. Miss Debenham says you've got into silly fights with some of the boys – and you really upset one of the girls yesterday. Judy someone?'

That was great. She was carrying on with this boring boring Noah's Ark nonsense and she'd just got started doing the giraffe's long neck with brown paint, so I got Garnet and we did our wanting-to-wee double act and then as we went out we both bumped into Judy accidentally on purpose and her giraffe ended up with this amazing corkscrew neck. Shame.

I couldn't help sniggering just thinking about it, and Dad got madder than ever.

Garnet spoilt it a bit because she started snivelling, as always. Then Dad sighed and said, 'Why do you always have to copy Ruby, Garnet? You obviously tried hard at school at first. But now you're starting to be just as naughty as Ruby.' And then he shook me a bit and said, 'Why can't you ever copy Garnet, Ruby?'

But Garnet was OK.

'I don't copy Ruby,' she said.

'I don't copy Garnet,' I said.

And then I sniffed because I knew Garnet was just about to, and I rubbed my dry eyes and she rubbed her wet ones, and then Garnet knew I'd stare at Dad defiantly with my chin up so she did too.

It unnerved Dad, even though he's used to us. But Rose clapped her hands.

'They ought to go on stage,' she said.

'Well ha ha ha, we're going to,' I said.

Garnet was a bit slow with her response this time. She only managed a '. . . going to,' and she sounded a bit half-hearted. But I'm her other half. The oldest biggest bossiest half. We have to do what I say.

EIGHT

This is it! Our Big Chance!

We were sitting in the kitchen on Saturday, mucking about. Dad was down in the shop. Rose had caught the early bus to the town. We had the place to ourselves. Garnet mixed up some flour and water and started making dinky little dough twins.

She even plaited their hair and gave them little laces in their trainers.

I said I wanted mine to have Doc Martens – all the better for kicking, ha ha – and I tried to change their shoes, but they wouldn't go right. So I squashed my twin up and started all over again, but it just went all blobby. I turned it into Jeremy Blob instead, while Garnet made another me. Then I got some toothpicks and tortured Jeremy Blob until he stopped looking like a doughboy and turned into a porcupine.

I got fed up with dough then and folded up

a newspaper and cut it out carefully the way Gran showed us once and then, when I unfolded it, there was this whole row of paper dolls. The newspaper just happened to be Rose's *Guardian* and she hadn't even opened it yet. Tough.

I got a felt tip and started scribbling in eyes and mouths and buttons down the front of each little paper girl. I'm not dead artistic like Garnet. I can't be bothered to be so finicky.

'I'm turning them all into twins,' I said.

I did a smily mouth for me and a little-o anxious mouth for Garnet, and then a smiley mouth for me and a . . .

And then I stopped, because I saw the word Twin on the paper doll. I read her skirt and then I ferreted around for the left-over paper to try to read the rest. I got the Sellotape and started trying to stick the whole bang-shoot back together again.

'Yes, Rose is going to want to read that when she gets back,' Garnet mumbled, putting the finishing touches to the little dough me.

'Blow Rose reading it. *We've* got to read it!' I said, and I was so shaking with excitement that I stuck myself together with the Sellotape. 'Garnet, come and take a look at this! Oh boy! No, oh *girl*. Oh *twin* girl!'

'Whatever are you burbling about?' said Garnet. 'Hey, don't jog. Look, you've made me muck up your plait now.'

'Leave it. *Look!*'

I shoved the crumpled, Sellotaped sheet of paper in front of her nose.

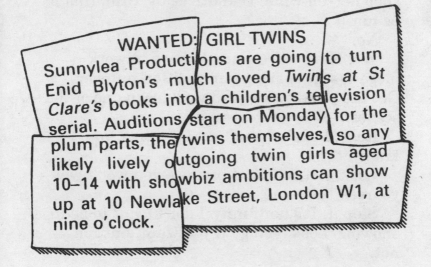

WANTED: GIRL TWINS
Sunnylea Productions are going to turn Enid Blyton's much loved *Twins at St Clare's* books into a children's television serial. Auditions start on Monday for the plum parts, the twins themselves, so any likely lively outgoing twin girls aged 10–14 with showbiz ambitions can show up at 10 Newlake Street, London W1, at nine o'clock.

'This is it, Garnet!' I shouted.

Garnet is usually a quick reader but she seemed to be taking her time getting through one small paragraph.

She was still holding the little dough me.

'Hey, watch out! You're spoiling me,' I said.

Garnet squashed me into a little ball and then dropped me on the kitchen floor.

'No,' she said.

'What?'

'No. I can't.'

'What do you *mean*? We can we can we can. Yes, all right, it's going to be difficult getting to London by nine o'clock. We'll have to get up ever so early. Rose will have to look after the shop herself while Dad drives us. Still, that'll be fun.'

'*No.*'

'Yes. Now, we're going to have to work mega-fast preparing our audition number. Get the book, quick, and we'll learn one of the scenes.'

'Ruby, I can't. I can't act for toffee, you know I can't.'

'Look, it'll be fine. I promise you won't wet yourself this time.'

'Stop it. It's not funny. I don't *want* to be in showbiz. Look, you go if you want, but I'm not.'

'Oh ha ha, very helpful. How can I audition as a twin by myself, eh? Take one of the little dough twins along with me? Don't be such a dope. Now, where's the book, we've got to get cracking. Which twin is which? I'll be the one that says the most. We'll work it so you don't have to say hardly anything, OK?'

'No, Ruby, please, *please*.' Garnet started scrabbling at me, getting dough all over my jumper.

'We can't miss out on this, Garnet. It's our big chance. We've got to go for it.'

'But it says lively. I'm not a bit lively. I don't jump about like you, I just sort of flop in a corner. And I'm not outgoing. I'm as inwardbeing as you could possibly get.'

'You'll be OK. Just copy me.'

Why do I always have to copy Ruby?
I can't act.
I don't want to act.
I can't go to an audition in London! I can't say a lot of stuff with everyone watching. It'll be even worse than being a sheep. Why won't Ruby understand? She won't listen to me. She's riffling through The Twins at St Clare's *right this minute, trying to choose which bit we'll act out.*

Only I'm not going to act.

I can't can't can't act.

Remember what Gran says? There's no such word as can't! Now stop scribbling and start spouting. We've got to be word-perfect by Monday!

It's OK! I don't have to act after all. Dad won't let us.

I can't believe he could be so Mega-Mean. He doesn't seem to see this is our one big chance, tailor-made for us. He won't even take it seriously.

'Don't be daft, Ruby. As if I'm going to drive you all the way to London at the crack of dawn on Monday! And I don't want you and Garnet involved in any acting caper while you're still children. I can't stick those simpering stage-school kiddiewinks. You're already enough of a show-off as it is.'

What a CHEEK! He can't be bothered to help us achieve our all-time ambition

Your *ambition*

and yet look what we've had to do for him. We've had to leave Gran and all our friends and our old school and come and live in this horrible dusty old dump in the middle of the boring bleak rainy old country which is all mud and sheep and nothing else and he says we've got to have old Rosy Ratbag as our *mother*.

Stepmother. And Rose said she didn't fancy herself as a stepmother anyway, and she didn't want us to feel she was forever trying to slip us poisoned apples. She said she just wanted to be our friend.

Well, we don't ever ever ever want to be friends with her. Do we? *Do we, Garnet?*

I suppose not. No. But she's not really as bad as all that. And she said she didn't see why we couldn't go to the audition. She said she thought we'd walk away with the parts.

She told Dad not to be so stuffy. She said she'd even get up early on Monday and drive us in the van.

Yes, but she didn't really mean it. She knew Dad would put his foot down and say no.

Still, she did stick up for us.

Look, what is this, the Rosy Ratbag Appreciation Society? You'll be writing a fanzine about her next.
Save your appreciation for *us*.

The talented gems of stage and screen, identical twins Ruby and Garnet Barker, who first sprang to stardom in the acclaimed television serial, 'The Twins at St Clare's.'

Only we're not going to be in The Twins at St Clare's.

Oh yes we are.

Dad won't let us. He won't ever change his mind. He's like you. He won't take us.

I know he won't take us. So we'll take ourself.

What???

I'll fix it. We *can't* miss this chance. Come on, Garnet. Twin-grin. *Smile.*

Ruby won't be able to fix it – will she???

I DID FIX IT!!!
I prodded my brainbox into action and charged out on Saturday afternoon to arrange things. I phoned the station to check on train times.
I went into the video shop and ordered the taxi for quarter past five on Monday morning. Mr Baines the video man is also the taxi man. *And* he's also a nosy old git who wanted to know why we were going to the station to catch the early train. I spun him this tale

about it being Gran's birthday. He seemed to take it for granted that Dad was going to be visiting her too.

Then I went to the nearest antique shop and tried to sell my silver locket and my wristwatch and a dopey old china baby doll that Gran gave me. I never liked it even when I was little. Garnet played with mine as well as hers. But the doll *was* mine. And the locket and the watch. But the antique shop lady wouldn't buy them. She said I had to have Mummy or Daddy with me.

Well, I haven't *got* a mummy. Or much of a dad.

I tried the next antique shop. No go. And the last one. Useless.

But did I give up? Nope. I went to the car-boot sale in the field by the river on Sunday morning. No-one was very interested in my chain and my watch but I saw them get excited about the doll, even though they tried to act like they couldn't be bothered. They offered me a fiver like they were doing me a favour. I'm not daft. I asked for fifty. Of course they didn't *give* me fifty. But they gave me twenty.

Which wasn't going to be enough for the taxi and the train fare, even with all our savings in our piggybank, so when my alarm

went off at four in the morning I sneaked
downstairs while Garnet was still asleep and
pinched a note or two out the till. It isn't
really stealing if it's your own family, is it? If
you're going to pay them back anyway? Well,
all right, it is – but I *had* to.

Then I went and woke Garnet and we
bumbled about in the dark getting ready, in
our best clothes

and then we crept downstairs and snaffled
some biscuits for breakfast and then stood
outside the front door waiting for Mr Baines
so that he wouldn't ring the bell and wake
Dad or Rosy Ratbag. They were still fast
asleep. I checked.

Mr Baines was ten minutes late so I was in a bit of a tizzy in case we were going to miss the train, and then he held things up by asking where Dad was, and he's got this incredibly loud voice and I was sure he was going to wake everyone up. But I rose to the occasion. I spun him this story about Dad having a tummy bug and being unable to travel, but Gran was so disappointed when he rang her that he promised to send us on our own.

'Two little girls like you?' said Mr Baines doubtfully, but I showed him my bulging purse and told him Gran was meeting us off the train, so he shrugged and said OK.

Garnet didn't say a word. She still seemed half-asleep. Then she went green in the taxi. *I'm* the one who gets travel-sick, but I was perfectly OK. I even remembered to give Mr Baines a tip, thought I didn't think he really deserved it, being late and asking hundreds of questions all the way.

I bought the tickets for the train. Garnet wasn't with me. She was being sick behind a hedge. I was worried she might muck up her best jacket. You can't audition attractively with vomit all down your front. But she was quite neat about it, though she looked greener than ever when she came back. Still, our jackets are green, so at least she matched.

She was all shivery, even on the train. I made her rehearse a bit and she got even more trembly and tearful.

'Don't you dare cry,' I said. 'You don't want to be all red-eyed and bleary at the audition.'

She did cry a bit even so, but I mopped her up in the ladies loo.

'You're not going to let me down, are you, Garnet?' I said very fiercely.

Sometimes you've got to be fierce to get what you want. But even I felt a bit timid when we got off the train because it was all so big and busy and we didn't know where to go and we asked someone where Newlake Street was and they'd never even heard of it, and I said we'd get a tube but we didn't know which tube, or where, and we went down the escalator and then back up the escalator and then I saw a taxi sign and we still had some money in our purse so we took a taxi.

It turned out we didn't have quite enough money after all. The taxi driver got a bit narked.

But I wasn't bothered about that. I was bothered about something else. I got out of the taxi and Garnet staggered out after me. And we stared. And hundreds of eyes stared back at us. Twin eyes. Twin after twin after twin after twin.

NINE

It was so weird seeing so many twins. Ruby and I have seen identical twins before, obviously, but never hundreds of pairs. It was as if the whole world had split into two. I felt as if I was splitting too. We've always felt so different. Unique. Special. It's what made us us. But standing there in that street we were just part of the crowd. Totally ordinary. With nothing at all to make us stand out.

'Let's go back home,' I said to Ruby. 'Look at them all. We don't stand a chance.'

'Don't be so ridiculous,' said Ruby furiously. 'I keep telling and telling and telling you, this is our big chance. We're not giving up now. We'll show them all. We'll act better than any of them.'

'But I can't act at all, Ruby.'

She just gave me this terrible look, took hold of my arm, and marched me to the end of the very long queue.

We passed big twins

little twins

pretty twins

plain twins

showy twins

shabby twins

girly-girly twins

tomboy twins

even real boy twins.

'They obviously haven't even read the book!' said Ruby dismissively. 'Unless they're going to put on frocks and wigs and play the parts in drag.'

'But look at some of the others. The ones with the big smiles and loud voices. I bet they've been to acting school,' I said.

'Well, so what. I've done my best to school you in acting. Now come on, let's go over our parts.'

'Not out here, in front of everyone,' I said, agonized.

'Look, you're the one who needs heaps of practice, not me,' said Ruby. Then she pulled me close and muttered in my ear, 'We'll just do it in whispers, OK? And I've been thinking – we'll have to inject a little ooomph into our act to make us stand out in front of all these others. So we'll still do the scene with the twins having a battle with Mam'zelle, but we'll act Mam'zelle too. Don't look so scared, I'll do her. I am good at doing zee French accent, ma cherie, oh la la, très bon.'

But it turned out we didn't get a chance to do any of our act. We had to wait hours and hours in the queue and I was desperate to go to the loo so when we did eventually get inside the building I had to walk around with my legs crossed and we had to give our names

and addresses and date of birth and school to
this lady at a desk and then we went upstairs
and I was scared I might really wet myself
and it would be the sheep situation all over
again only worse but there were toilets along
the corridor

and a big cloakroom where you were supposed
to change only we didn't have anything to
change into, 'cos we were wearing it. But Ruby
pinched my cheeks to give me a bit more
colour and I tidied our hair although my
hands were trembling so I could barely tie a
knot and then we got into another queue,

waiting to get into the actual audition room.

It got scarier and scarier and I had to dash back to the loo once or twice and even Ruby got a bit fidgety and she kept staring round at all the other twins. They were rehearsing their routines and they all seemed so brilliant

that Ruby started to frown and bite her nails.

'I didn't figure we might have to dance,' she mumbled. 'They don't do any dancing in the story do they? Although maybe they're turning it into a musical version? So if we're asked, we'll sing . . . er . . . not a pop song, they'll all do that. We could do "My Bonnie Lies Over the Ocean" with hand gestures.'

'I'm not singing, especially not with gestures!' I said. 'You know we can't sing in tune, either of us.'

'Well, we could just sort of say the words, with lots of expression,' said Ruby relentlessly. 'And if we have to dance well . . . we'll just have to jump and jiggle a bit. Improvise. You copy me, OK?'

This was so obviously not OK that I didn't even bother to protest.

'We could work on a routine now, you know,' said Ruby, hopping and skipping and kicking out one leg.

She kicked a little too enthusiastically, and there was an argument with the twins in front of us.

They were dressed up in wonderfully old-fashioned school uniform – gymslips and baggy blouses and lisle stockings and strappy shoes. One of the lisle stockings had a little ladder now where it had connected with Ruby's kick, and the mother of the laddered-lisle was very cross indeed.

'Look, it was an accident – anyway, it just adds to her general schoolgirl . . .authenticity,' said Ruby, pronouncing this big word with pride.

The mother didn't seem convinced, and the schoolgirl twins were still getting all shirty too, but then they were called into the audition room so they rushed off in a fluster.

'Us next,' said Ruby. She took hold of me by the shoulders. 'We're going to do great, Garnet. Better than any of this dopey stupid showy-offy lot. You and me. Ruby and Garnet. We'll act it all out and it won't be scary at all, it'll just be like us playing in private at home. Trust me.'

I tried. And then it was our turn. And it wasn't at all like playing in private. We were shown on to this stage and there were lots of people watching us and a camera filming us and I was so frightened I nearly fell over. Ruby grabbed me by the hand and hissed 'Twin-grin' and marched us into the middle of the stage.

'Hi, twins,' said this woman with short hair and a smock.

'Hi there,' said Ruby, imitating her voice, trying to sound all cool and casual, though I could see little beads of sweat on her forehead.

She nudged me, and I squeaked 'Hi' too.

'We've got our audition piece all prepared,' Ruby said brightly, trying to show them we were dead professional. 'I'm Pat and she's Isabel and I'm also Mam'zelle and at the end I'm Janet as well.'

They all laughed, for some reason. I blushed, because I was scared they thought Ruby was silly, but Ruby didn't seem to mind. She laughed too.

'We'd love to see your little number some time, twins, but right now we just want to test out your voices,' said the woman with the short hair. 'Sooo – twin number one. Tell me what you had to eat yesterday.'

Ruby blinked at her. But then she threw back her hair, put her hand on one hip, and got started.

'OK, you want to know what I had to eat yesterday. Well, breakfast was boring old muesli again. Garnet and I used to have Coco Pops and jam sandwiches and they were yummy, but now we have this awful woman living with us, our dad's girlfriend, and she's into health foods so it's bye-bye Coco Pops, hello muesli – all this oat and bran that makes your face ache munching and then there are these little raisins like rabbit droppings, yuck.'

They were all laughing again, but this time even I could see that this was good. They loved Ruby.

'Right, now, twin two, tell us what you had for lunch,' said the woman with short hair.

They stopped looking at Ruby. They looked at me. And Ruby looked at me too. Desperately. Terrified I was going to let us down.

I tried to pretend to myself that I wasn't shy

*stupid scaredy-cat Garnet. I made out I was
Ruby. I threw back my hair. I put my hand on
my hip. I opened my mouth to start.*

*I had it all worked out what I was going to
do. I was going to tell about Rose's garlic
crumble and how it not only tasted absolutely
disgusting, but people ducked and dodged for
days afterwards whenever we breathed in
their direction and we'd worn out six
toothbrushes already trying to take the taste
away. I could be funny too if I really tried. I
could be just as good as Ruby. I could.*

*But then someone came bursting through
the door and stood there, staring.* Dad!

And I couldn't. I simply couldn't.

He didn't say anything to stop me.

*But he didn't need to. I couldn't get started,
not in front of him. I opened my mouth – but
nothing came out. I tried to speak, but I
couldn't even squeak.*

'Come on, *Garnet,' said Ruby.*

*I gulped, I opened my mouth, I tried. But
all I managed was a goldfish impersonation.*

*'Look, I'll say what we had for lunch,' said
Ruby.*

*'No, sweetie, we've already heard you. We
want your twin to talk now. Let's skip lunch.
And tea and supper. What time did you go to
bed, twin two?'*

I saw Ruby flash her eyes at me. I knew she was willing me to tell a funny story about our bed-delaying tactics, our constant unnecessary trips to the bathroom, our midnight raids on the fridge, our frequent nocturnal ramblings – all deliberately done to unnerve Dad and Rose, so that they could never totally relax into unwedded bliss.

I could tell it, but not in front of Dad.

So, after several centuries had gone by and I actually saw the short-haired woman glance at her watch, I started a stupid mumble about 'Well, we're supposed to start getting ready for bed at nine, ten at weekends, but we often try to stay up.'

My voice was this sad expressionless little squeak. I saw Ruby close her eyes in agony. I saw Dad hang his head. I saw the short-haired woman and all her colleagues shaking their heads. I saw it all and I shrank down to mouse-size to match my squeak.

'Thank you, sweetie. Off you go, twins. Next!' said the short-haired woman. She was already staring past us, smiling at the new set of twins.

'No, hang on a minute!' said Ruby. 'Look my sister isn't very well, she's been sick, she's not normally like this, she can speak up and be ever so funny, I swear she can. How about if we just do a couple of minutes of our prepared piece? Give us a chance. We've used up all our savings getting here, and we're going to get in terrible trouble with our dad when we get back . . .'

'Yes, it's a shame, sweetie, but we don't really have the time,' said the short-haired woman, and she put her arm round both of us. It wasn't just sympathy. She propelled us gently but firmly to the edge of the stage.

Even in the midst of her despair Ruby remembered the camera, twisting round and grimacing in agony, and then she sighed and waved her hand.

I could hear a few chuckles.

'That kid's a caution,' said someone.

'Yeah. Pity about her twin.'

It was only a murmur. But it was like a giant roaring in my ears. It wouldn't soften or stop.

I couldn't seem to hear properly even when Dad caught up with us.

'You bet you're in terrible trouble,' he said furiously. 'How dare you run off here like this, when I expressly forbade it. I couldn't believe it when we woke up and found you both gone. I was so worried I was going to call the police, but Rose insisted you'd both be all right and that you'd obviously gone for this idiotic audition.'

'Well, it was a complete waste of time anyway,' said Ruby. 'You really blew it for us, Dad. We were doing just great and then you had to come barging in and put us off our stroke.'

'Put me off. Not you,' I said. 'And it wasn't Dad's fault. He waited. He gave us a chance. But I mucked it up. That's what they said. You were great, Ruby, yeah. But I was useless. They said so.'

'No they didn't,' said Ruby. 'And anyway, they didn't give you a proper chance. It wasn't fair.'

'You don't want to be an actress anyway, Garnet,' said Dad. 'And even if you'd both been offered the parts, I wouldn't have let you take them. Ruby can act when she grows up, but I don't want my girls turning into

ghastly little child stars, thank you very much.'

'There's no chance of me being any sort of star,' I said, and I started crying. I couldn't bear it. They were both so sorry for me. Dad was still mega-mad because we'd sneaked off up to London by ourselves, but he was holding back his anger for a bit to try to comfort me.

And Ruby wasn't cross with me. She should hate me for ever because I did muck it up. I should have said all that stuff and never mind about Dad being there. I could *have* done. Only I didn't. I let her down. I'll always let her down.

She's the biggest and the brightest and the best.

She's the caution.

She's the star.

It's a pity she's stuck with me.

Pity about her twin.

Pity about her twin.

Pity about her twin.

TEN

What's all this pity piffle??? Perlease, Garnet!
And anyway, I did get cross with you. I had a
real go at you in the car, because you *were* a
bit of a wally at the audition. What did it
matter if Dad was there or not? You could
have made something up if you didn't want to
do a rant at Rose. I mean, I wouldn't go on at
you if I truly thought you couldn't do it, but
you *can*. Well, you could have. Only it's too
late now. We've blown it. Lost our chance. We
don't get to be famous child stars. We're drab
child nobodies stuck in this dreary dump for
ever and ever. *And* we've lost all our savings
for nothing. Not to mention my baby doll that
Gran gave me.

Garnet? Oh, don't start crying *again*.

Look, *I'm* the one who should be crying.
I'm the one who wants to act. *I'm* the one that
Dad is maddest at. The way he went on and
on at me! And then when I argued back and

told him he was an old worryguts and that we're big enough to look after ourselves and what possible harm could happen on a simple trip to London, I thought he was actually going to clock me one.

He hasn't ever smacked us, has he? I wish he would, then we could show the bruises at school and get taken into care.

I mean it. I'm sick of living here with him and her.

Hey, let's write to Gran and see if she could possibly squeeze us into her flat. We could sleep curled up on her settee, couldn't we? And she keeps saying how much she misses us on her postcards.

Then we could go back to our old school. We're not going to this stupid new school again, especially now that Dumbo Debenham's told tales on us. We're not going even if Dad picks us up and tries to drag us there. We're not speaking to him, right? And we're certainly not speaking to *Rose*. Who cares if she came out with all that guff about us being ultra-determined and clever getting ourselves to London. We didn't ask her to stick up for us, did we?

Garnet? Look, what does it matter what she's shouting? We don't want to go and watch television with her! Who cares if it's—

It was us! Well, only a glimpse, but they showed me, doing my goodbye bit. The camera came right up close. They didn't show much of Garnet, just a bit of her hair and an elbow but they showed all of me, and there was a voice-over saying, 'And this twin certainly took rejection like a trouper.'

Pity they didn't say our names. Still. We were on the telly. Well, I was.

It was on the News. We missed the first part but Rose videoed it. They did a whole little item about the audition for the *Twins at St Clare's* series as a clever early puff for the programme, seeing as it's going to be made by the same telly company. They showed some of those other twins doing their party pieces. There weren't any as good as us. Well, me. Of course, that's only my opinion.

The twins that they've chosen are absolutely *awful*.

That's the way they talk,too. Oooh absolutely jolly good show, fwightfully, ya, jolly super-duper green-welly wallies.

Perhaps it's just as well we weren't chosen. If they'd got us to talk all twiddly-snooty-pop like that then we'd have been sent up rotten for ever and a day. Kids won't want to watch a pathetic programme like that. Or if they do, they'll just laugh at it.

Still, it looks like they're pulling out all the stops on the production. It's being filmed on location in this real big boarding school during the summer holidays. They showed all the grounds. It was just like a stately home. And there was a swimming pool. And a sort of

miniature zoo, where they keep their pets.
And inside this huge great house it wasn't a
bit like a *school* school. There were ordinary
boring old classrooms but they had playrooms
with television and videos and music centres
and computers and upstairs there weren't
dormitories like I thought – they had lots of
bedrooms with flowery duvets and teddies on
the beds and posters up on the walls, and
best of all, this school has its own *theatre*. It's
quite small, OK, but it's got a real stage with
red velvet curtains and lighting and props
and everything, and they put on plays.

I wish we could go to a school like that.

Hey.

Wow.

Yes!

No!

Oh, Garnet, come on! It would be absolutely
fantastic! Oh, let's go there. We wouldn't be
acting, we'd be the *real* twins of St Clare's.
Well, Marnock Heights. It would be such fun.
We could play all those posh games – hockey
and lacrosse and cricket in the summer. I bet
I'd be absolutely ace at cricket. And we could
have a pet each in the little zoo place. Twin
pets.

Rabbits? Those little ones with shy faces. Dwarf rabbits.

OK, twin baby bunnies. Though I'd sooner have gerbils. Or rats.

I don't like rats. Or gerbils. I don't even like mice.

Right, we're agreed. It's rabbits. We'll go and play with our rabbits every day and we'll have a game of cricket and we'll swim in the pool and in the evenings we'll watch videos in the sitting-room and then, after we've gone to bed, we'll have mega-midnight feasts.

This is a game, isn't it?

No! It can be real. We're going to go to boarding school.

Yes, it's a school, so there'll be lessons all day. We can't just muck about stroking our rabbits and playing games. There'll be English and History and Technology. And hard stuff too like Geometry and Latin.

That's OK. You'll be able to do that. And did

you see that library in the telly clip? All those wonderful books, Garnet.

We've got books here.

Old boring books. We hate this bookshop. We hate this school and this whole horrible dump of a village. So we're going to get out. We're going to go to boarding school. Marnock Heights. We'll write a letter applying. You'd better do it, Garnet, your writing's much neater than mine. I'll tell you what to put.

But I don't want to—

I'm sick of you going on about what you want and don't want. Look, *I* wanted to be one of the twins of St Clare's on the television. *I* planned and plotted so that we got all the way to London by ourselves. *I* sold all my stuff. *I* did my audition thingy so well that they all laughed and they really liked me, and it looked like we'd actually got the part, didn't it? But then *you* mucked it up.

Yes.

There's no need to look like that. I'm not being deliberately horrid. I'm just trying to get you to understand that it would be ultra ultra ultra mean of you to muck up my chances of getting what I want second best in the world. Right?

The Red Bookshop
High Street
Cussop

19 May

Dear Madam - We are sorry, we don't know your name.

We are ten-year-old identical twins, nearly eleven and we hate our school in this village. We don't fit in. The lessons are boring and there aren't any proper books and the only games we play are rounders.

We went to the television audition for _The Twins at St Clare's_. We very nearly got the part actually. We were featured in the television coverage. Well, one of us was. And you were featured too and your wonderful school and we thought Oooh this is our idea of heaven, the stage and the swimming pool and the games and the animals and all that.

So please can we come to your school in September? We promise to be good pupils and you don't have to worry about us being homesick because we hate our home. Yours faithfully

Ruby Barker
Garnet Barker.

P.S. Please say yes. You won't regret it. Honestly.

Look at this!

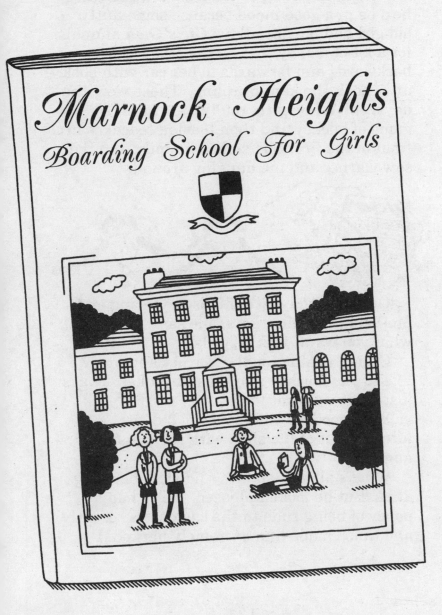

We went rushing to tell Dad. We thought he'd be in a good mood because some nutty old girl had bought all his *Girls' Own* annuals for a lot of money, and as she staggered backwards and forwards to her car with book after book she kept burbling, 'Those were the days, eh? When girls really *were* girls. A hard game of hockey and then toasted teacakes in front of the fire.' She sighed happily, and then saw Garnet and me hanging around.

'Only nowadays it's all disco dancing and McDonald's beefburgers,' she said. 'That's what you want, isn't it, girls?'

'Oh no,' I said quickly. 'Garnet and me, we'd like to play hockey and toast teacakes. That's just what we want too.'

'Well, good for you,' said the old girl, lurching out of the shop with the last of her annuals.

'What's all this about?' said Dad, blinking at us. But he looked pleased. We've had a policy of being rude to the customers recently and that's made him extremely narked. I looked at Garnet. She looked at me. I took a deep breath.

'We're not kidding, Dad. We read all the *St Clare's* books, see, when we were wanting to act in the telly series. And we think it all sounds really great. So Garnet and I want to go to boarding school.'

Dad laughed, not taking us seriously.

'It's not really like it is in books,' said Dad. 'I don't think either of you would go a bundle on real boarding school. You have to work hard and do as you're told all the time. According to poor Miss Debenham, you don't do any work at all and never ever do as you're told.'

'Yes, but that's because she's a silly teacher and it's a silly school. But if we went to a super top-notch boarding school then we'd be mega-good, really truly. A boarding school like Marnock Heights.'

'Like *where?*'

'It's the place they're using for the *St Clare's* film. It's a real school. And so Garnet and I wrote to the headmistress asking to go there and she's sent us this booklet all about it, look.'

I ran to fetch it and shoved it under Dad's nose.

'Oh, for goodness sake! Will you girls *stop*

135

doing things behind my back,' Dad groaned.

'Say we can go, though, Dad, *please*. You look at all the pictures. It's lovely, isn't it?'

'Oh, very lovely,' said Dad, flicking through. Then he stopped at the back page, where there were two pieces of paper tucked into a little pocket. 'And very lovely school fees too! Eight thousand a year. Each! Oh yes, nice one, Ruby.'

I stared at him and then snatched the paper. There were all these figures on it. The fees. I didn't realize you had to *pay* to go to some schools. You had to pay an enormous enormous enormous fee to go to Marnock Heights.

'Oh no,' I wailed.

'Oh no,' Garnet wailed too. But she didn't sound too fussed, in actual fact. Right, Garnet????

Well . . .

We've got to think POSITIVE. Because all is not lost. Maybe Dad won't have to fork out any fees. Not that he could anyway. We're far too poor. But But But . . . There was a letter tucked into the pocket of the prospectus, along with the note about the frightful fees.

136

                    Marnock Heights
                    Gorselea
                    Sussex

                    22 May

Dear Ruby and Garnet

     What lovely names! You wrote me a
lovely letter too. I'm pleased that you'd
like to attend Marnock Heights. Here is
the current prospectus. Show it to your
parents or guardians.
     I'd like to point out that we do
award several special scholarships each
year. These have already been awarded for
the new intake in the Autumn, but one
girl is now unable to take up her
scholarship because she's going abroad.
Perhaps you would like to come to the
school and sit the entrance examination
to see if either of you might pass highly
enough for scholarship consideration?
     Please telephone my secretary for
an appointment.

With best wishes

Yours sincerely

Miss Jeffreys

Headteacher
(There, you know my name now!)

ELEVEN

Dad still wouldn't hear of it. At first. But we kept on at him.

You *kept on at him.*

On and on and on. And then he started to weaken.

It was Rose too. She said we should go for it. She said she wished she'd had a proper education.
'It's a great chance. It's ever such a famous school. If one of them got a scholarship there then they'd be able to go on, do anything, achieve anything.'

She's just desperate to get rid of us. Because we're driving her crackers.

You sometimes drive me crackers, Ruby. You won't ever change your mind about anyone.

Or anything. So we're going to Marnock Heights!

We're sitting the exam, that's all. And I don't see the point, as there's two of us and only one scholarship.

We'll wangle two, somehow. Once Miss Jeffreys gets to know us. She likes us already. She's ever so complimentary in her letter. We're lovely. I'm Miss Lovely Ruby and you're Miss Lovely Garnet, OK? Oh, come *on*, Garnet, cheer up! We've won! We've got our own way!

You've got your own way. And I'm worried about the exam. She doesn't say what sort. If it's an interview then I'm scared I'll go all stupid and shy and not know what to say. Like at the audition.

It's OK, I'll do all the talking. You just leave it to me.

So I left the talking to Ruby. We were shown into Miss Jeffreys' study and she shook our hands and smiled and gave us tea and biscuits and as we sipped and nibbled, Miss Jeffreys asked us questions.

They were really hard questions too, like:

'Why do you think education for girls is important?'

and 'What are your ambitions for the future?'

and 'What do you like doing in your spare time?'

and even 'How do you feel about being a twin?'

I feel bad about being a twin because I let Ruby down. I couldn't think of a thing to say. I just tagged on to the end of her sentences. She was brilliant.

Hmm! *Mega*-brilliant.

It was easy-peasy. I didn't say what I *really* think, naturally. I just said all this stuff to impress Miss Jeffreys and make her see that we are ideal pupils for Marnock Heights. I don't care a bit about education but I spouted stuff that old Rosy-Ratbag said the other day. And I said truthfully enough that our ambition is to be famous actresses, but I said we needed to study Shakespeare and if we stay in Cussop you don't even get *started* on Shakespeare until you go to sixth-form college. And I said that in our spare time we acted, and we also read lots, and I named all the books that Garnet likes, and some of Dad's Dickens and Hardy, and Miss Jeffreys looked dead impressed. She asked about the stories but I made some stuff up and I'm sure she swallowed it. And then when she asked about the twin bit I said it was just like being one person, only we were twice as good as anyone else.

She laughed and said that was a really good answer.

So *I* said that it was ever so important that we mustn't ever be separated and that as we always shared everything maybe we could share a scholarship too.

Dad got all fidgety then but she laughed even more. Then she took us all round the

school and the grounds, and it is truly
fantastic.

The other girls seem OK too. One looked a
bit snobby so I stuck my tongue out at her,
but she stuck her tongue out back at me and
then we both grinned. She had red hair and
little wicked eyes. I think we'll be friends
with her when we come to Marnock Heights.

If.

Look, I keep *telling* you, Garnet, we'll get
there. OK, we had to sit in the library and do
that boring old written exam – and I must
admit that got me a bit worked up because

143

that other teacher insisted that we sit at opposite ends so we couldn't work together the way we always do. That was ever so unfair. And then, when I caught your eye and we were sort of conferring, it was mean of that teacher to make me turn round and face the other way. They don't understand. We weren't cheating or anything. It's just the way we work, isn't it? Especially when it comes to all that boring stuff like arithmetic and general knowledge. And that composition was ultra-blobby-boring. 'Snow in Winter'! What did you write, eh?

You'll get mad at me.

Oh no. What did you put???

I just imagined a mountain all over with snow and what it must look like. And how odd it must be for the sheep, all green grass one minute and then white sharp stuff that hurts their teeth. And people always say there's a blanket of snow on the ground and yet if you were under that blanket, buried, you'd be dead. And how once when we were making snow angels in the park I stopped moving my arms and legs to see what it would feel like to be frozen. And snow looks so clean and pure

but nothing's dirtier when everyone's trudged
through it and it's all grey with yellow patches
and how it's always like that, it can't ever stay
the same, and yet each time you hope there'll
be a way of keeping it looking beautiful.

Oh yucky yucky yuck! What did you have
to write that rubbish for? I just bunged a few
bits down about robins and icicles and
footsteps crunching, like the verses inside
Christmas cards. That's what they wanted,
you idiot, not all your weirdo ramble.

I'm sorry, Ruby.

Yes, well, so you should be.

Ruby . . . What if you get accepted for the
scholarship and I don't?

We're *both* going to get a scholarship.

But what if we don't? Would you go to
Marnock Heights without me?

I keep telling and telling you, we're going
together.

Yes, and I keep asking and asking . . . if it's

just you that gets accepted, will you go?

No. Yes. I don't *know.*

I think you should. Though it will be horrible without you. But I can't stand it if I'm always going to be the one that holds you back.

Marnock Heights

Gorselea
Sussex
29 May

Dear Mr Barker

I thoroughly enjoyed meeting you and your delightful daughters last week.

Ruby is a charming child, so full of vim and vigour. No wonder she wants to be an actress. I am sure she will succeed in her ambitions one day. I'm afraid we can't offer her a scholarship at Marnock Heights. She is obviously witty and intelligent and her conversation sparkles – though she tends to get rather carried away and bluffs when she's uncertain! Her written work is lively if a little slapdash, but I'm afraid she failed several of our tests. If she could only apply herself more vigorously then I'm sure she could reach a far

We're not going to be held back, either of us. We're going rushing forwards. To Marnock Heights.

higher standard. I feel she's relied on her sister to do all her work for so long that she's failed to reach her full academic potential.

Garnet too might benefit from a term of separation from her sister. She lets Ruby do all her talking for her, and therefore does not interview at all well. However, she came into her own in the written tests. She has a few gaps in her knowledge but on the whole she did very well. Her essay was outstanding – extremely sensitive and mature. We would like to offer her a full scholarship at Marnock Heights, commencing in the Autumn term.

With best wishes

Yours sincerely

Miss Jeffreys

Headteacher

TWELVE

We couldn't believe it. We thought Miss Jeffreys had got us mixed up.

'She means me,' said Ruby. 'She must mean me.'

'Yes, it can't be me,' I said. 'Ruby will have got the scholarship.'

'No,' said Dad. 'It's definitely Garnet.'

'Let me see the letter!' Ruby demanded.

Dad didn't want either of us to see it.

'It's addressed to me,' he said. 'And it's plain what it says. There's no mix up.'

'She's just got our names round the wrong way,' Ruby insisted. 'It's always happening.'

'Not this time,' said Rose.

'Look, it's absolutely not fair if she's read the letter too, when it's got nothing to do with her. She's not our mother,' said Ruby.

'No, but I'm your father, and I want you to calm down, Ruby, and we'll talk all this over carefully.'

'Not till you show me the letter!'

'I'd show both the girls the letter,' said Rose. 'They're not little kids. I think they should see what it says.'

So Dad showed us.

It was like a smack in the face.

Not for me. For Ruby.

I read quicker than she does. I watched her face while she was finishing the letter. I couldn't bear it.

'She's written a whole load of rubbish,' I said quickly. 'She only met us for one afternoon and yet she thinks she knows us. Well she doesn't, does she, Ruby?'

Ruby was getting very red in the face. She screwed her eyes up. She looked as if she was trying hard not to cry. But Ruby never cries.

'Ruby,' I said, and I put my arm round her.

She wriggled away as if my arm had turned into a snake.

'Oh, Ruby,' I said, and I was the one who started crying. 'Look, I'm not going to go to Marnock Heights. I didn't even want to go in the first place. It was you that wanted to, not me.'

I was making it worse.

'I think you should go, Garnet,' said Rose. 'You've done very well. We should all be busy congratulating you. I know it's tough on Ruby, but—'

'You don't know anything,' I shouted.

I couldn't stand it. I didn't want them ganging up on my side. I was on Ruby's side.

'Hey, we'll have less of that cheeky tone,' said Dad. 'Rose, love, could you make us all a cup of coffee? Let's talk it over, eh? It's been a bit of a shock for all of us. Ruby? Ruby, where are you going?'

'There's nothing to talk about,' said Ruby. Her voice sounded awful. She was trying to make it sound couldn't-care-less, but it kept catching in her throat. 'Garnet's got the scholarship. I haven't . And that's it.'

'But I'm not going, Ruby! Please believe me. I promise I'm not going to go. I couldn't stand going there. Especially without you.'

'So why did you try ever so hard in all those silly tests and write all that yucky stuff for your essay?' said Ruby.

'I don't know. I just didn't think. Oh, Ruby, I'm sorry.'

I tried to grab hold of her again but she wouldn't let me.

'You get away from me,' she said, ducking.

'Now this is getting ridiculous,' said Dad. 'Pull yourself together, Ruby. I'm ashamed of you. I know you've had a bit of a disappointment, but there's no need to be nasty to poor old Garnet. Why can't you be big enough to congratulate her? She didn't act like this over that television audition, now did she? She was full of praise for you.'

Dad was making it worse. I saw Ruby's eyes, as she ducked. They were brimming over.

'Oh, congratulations, clever goody-goody Garnet,' Ruby gabbled, and then she rushed out the room.

I tried to follow her, but Dad stopped me.

'No, Garnet. Let her go. She won't want you around for a bit, especially as she's crying,' he said. Perhaps he did understand a little bit after all. 'But there's no need for you to cry, sweetheart. Rose is right. You've done brilliantly and I'm very proud of you.'

'I'm not going though,' I wept.

'Well. I can't make you go. And this boarding school lark certainly wasn't my idea.

But I do think now that it's a wonderful opportunity.'

'I'll say,' said Rose, handing round the coffee. 'You've got to go for it, Garnet.'

'I can't leave Ruby,' I wailed.

'But Ruby would leave you,' said Rose.

'That's different,' I said.

'But it shouldn't be different,' said Dad, and he pulled me on to his lap. 'This letter has made me see that maybe it's bad for you and Ruby to be together all the time. You're holding each other back, spoiling each other's chances. You're growing up now, and you need to develop as two separate sisters.'

'But we're not separate. We're twins. We can't do without each other.'

'You're going to have to learn to some day,' said Dad. 'You'll both grow up and have different jobs and have different lifestyles and have different families.'

'No, we're going to stay together,' I said.

We'd got it all sorted out.

We'd stick together when we were young

and when we were old

and when we were even older

and if we ever wanted to get married then we'd marry twins

and have twin babies

*and then when they grew up they could
stick together for ever and maybe they'd have
twins too and then they could . . .*

*My head was buzzing with all these twins. I
wanted my own twin. I could hear her
upstairs. She was sobbing.*

I don't know what to do.

*It's worse than when Ruby wasn't talking to
me.*

She's talking now, but not properly. *And
she only talks when we're with other people.
When we're together she hardly says anything.
She won't play any of our games. She won't
plan any twin-tricks so that we do things
simultaneously.*

*She doesn't seem to want to be a twin any
more.*

*She won't even dress like me now. She waits
until she sees what I'm putting on and then
she puts on something entirely different. And
she does her hair in a new way too.*

I tried to copy her, so she changed it again.

And so I changed too. And then she did something terrible. She got the scissors and I thought she was bluffing. And then I wasn't sure.

'Don't!' I said.

But she did. She cut off all her hair.

'Oh Ruby, what have you done?' I said, looking at her poor head with the chopped hair sticking up like a scrubbing brush.

'I'm making me different,' she said, running

her hand through the stubble. She swallowed and sniffed. 'And you needn't look like that. I like it. I wanted it this way for ages. It's . . . sort of punk. Great.'

I didn't know what to do. We've always had long hair, right from when we were little. When Gran made us have plaits I would always do Ruby's as well as my own. Sometimes when I was feeling sleepy I'd forget which was my head and which was hers.

Now when I stared at Ruby I felt as if my own hair had been hacked off even though I could still feel the warm weight of it on my shoulders. It gave me the weirdest out-of-synch feeling, like when you watch a film and the people say things a fraction before their lips open.

Ruby couldn't grow her hair. So there was only one thing to do.

'No you don't!' Ruby hissed, as I reached for the scissors. She snatched them away from me. 'I'm warning you, Garnet. You cut off your hair and I'll cut off your head!'

She looked so fierce I felt I believed her. She looked like she hated me.

She took the scissors and some newspaper and cut out a line of paper dolls. She cut them into twins. And then she chopped through their hands, so they were separate.

She chopped so violently that they tore all the way up their arms.

It's me again. Ruby won't write in the book any more. I don't want to write much either. How can I give an account of us when we aren't us any more.

If only I could tear out all the pages about the school and the scholarship – scrub them out so that they never happened.

Ruby's acting like she wants to scrub me out altogether. It's the holidays now, but she won't go around with me. She just goes off by herself and when I try to follow her she runs away. She could always run faster than me. And she's better at hiding. I don't know where she goes or whether she joins up with anyone else. But she won't join up with me.

I asked her in bed at night if we could go back to being us if I wrote a letter to Miss Jeffreys saying I wasn't going to Marnock Heights.

I waited. The room was very dark but I could see her eyes open, watching me. She waited too.

Then she said into the silence, 'I don't care if you go or not, Garnet. You do what you like. And I'll do what I like. But we're not us any more and we can't ever be. We'll still be split up even if we stay together.'

But it's not what I like. I don't know what I like.

I don't want to go to Marnock Heights. Although I've been reading all these books. Not the twins ones. I feel sick whenever I see them. No, there's a whole shelf of old school stories at the back of the shop – girls who go to schools in Abbeys and Chalets and Towers – and I've been reading one in the morning and one in the afternoon and sometimes one in the evening too and sometimes – just sometimes – it sounds as if it might be fun.

Judy thinks so. She's dead envious. She comes round to the shop sometimes. I've been to tea at her house. She's got all these tapes and videos. You just have to sit and watch and listen. Or we go up to her bedroom and play games. Not *our* sort of games. Board games. And I do get a bit bored playing them. Judy's OK but she's a bit boring too.

She says she's seen Ruby going around with Jeremy Treadgold and his gang! Ruby with the Giant Blob??? I asked Ruby but she just rubbed the end of her nose, indicating that I should mind my own business.

Ruby doesn't want to be my business any more.

She's made herself different.

She even looks different.

People maybe wouldn't even think we were twins now.

Gran nearly did her nut when she came to stay for the weekend. This old man, Albert, drove her in his car. He's her neighbour in her sheltered flats. He came and stayed too, which made it a bit of a squash. Gran said we should call him Uncle Albert, though he's not our uncle.

I looked at Ruby and she looked at me and just for a second it was almost like the old days.

But these are new days and everything's changing and Ruby's changed most of all.

'WhatEVER have you done to yourself, Ruby???' Gran demanded. 'What DO you look like? You're such a scruff. Like a gutter child. And your HAIR! Oh my lord, have you got nits?'

'Leave off, Gran,' said Ruby, fidgeting and scowling.

'For goodness sake, how could you let her run round like a ragamuffin?' Gran said to Rose.

Rose had tried to smarten Ruby up a bit for Gran's visit. She'd washed all her best clothes and ironed them and she'd begged Ruby to let her try to neaten up her new hairstyle. Ruby refused. She wore her oldest dirtiest clothes and deliberately fished her old holey trainers out of the dustbin, even though Rose had bought her brand-new ones specially.

But Rose didn't say any of this.

'Ruby likes to be comfy. And we think her hairstyle really suits her, don't we, Ricky?'

'Sure,' said Dad, putting his arm round Rose.

'Well, at least Garnet looks fairly presentable,' Gran sniffed. 'But what's all this I hear about you being packed off to boarding school, Garnet? I don't hold with that idea at all. What's the matter, do they want to get rid of you?'

'Of course we don't want to get rid of her!' said Dad. 'We just think she should give it a try for a term, seeing as she's got this scholarship. But if she hates it then of course she can come home whenever she wants.'

But like I said, I still don't know what I want. I'm starting to get nightmares about going to the school.

And yet it's horrid at home now that Ruby is a stranger instead of a sister. I'd secretly hoped that I could talk to Gran in secret and ask her if I could maybe go and live with her for a bit – but I'd forgotten how naggy and niggly she can be sometimes. And then there's Albert who isn't our uncle. He's not part of our family but it looks as if he and Gran are a new family all of their own.

Then there's Dad and Rose. They have rows sometimes but they always make it up and when Rose tried ever so hard to cook a proper Sunday lunch for everyone, but somehow the beef got burnt and the Yorkshire pudding sulked and the potatoes wouldn't roast and

*the beans went stringy and the gravy had
lumps, Dad still ate up every scrap on his*

*plate and said it was super and even asked for
seconds.*
   They're a family too.

I'm part of their family and Gran's family and I used to have Mum as special family but even more than Mum there was always Ruby.
Ruby-and-Garnet.
Only now there's just Ruby. And Garnet.

Ruby?

Ruby.

Oh, Ruby.

MEMORANDUM

THIRTEEN

This is my written work. And I don't give a toss if it's slapdash. Who cares what that stupid jumped-up jelly-belly Jeffreys says?

I wouldn't want to go there anyway. Not now. I'm having heaps better fun here. I am.

Anyway, I bet Garnet doesn't have the bottle to go without me.

Or if she does, I bet she gets terribly homesick and cries heaps and will be sent back a sodden wreck.

She can't manage without me. Even she knows that.

But I'm doing just fine without her.

This is my new notebook and I shall take heaps of notes. It says MEMORANDUM on the cover. I like the first two letters. ME ME ME ME ME ME ME ME ME ME ME ME ME ME ME ME ME.

This notebook is going to be all about Me.

I like being just me.

I like it just me. Oh, I've put that bit before. Never mind. It makes it twice as true. I feel GREAT.

I know what Memorandum means, too. I am quite intelligent actually, even if some people seem to think I'm a total thicko. Memorandum means notes of things to be remembered. And I want it officially down on paper that

1. Ruby Barker doesn't give two hoots about not getting that stupid scholarship.

2. Ruby Barker doesn't give two hoots that her sneaky sister is going instead of her.

3. Ruby Barker doesn't give two hoots about said sneaky sister.

She is *absolutely devastated* (there, *I'm* the one who uses ever such posh long grown-up words, so it just goes to show that Miss Jeffreys is talking RUBBISH).

Yuck! Now. Where was I?

Oh yes. Garnet is truly despairing because I have broken up our twinship. She needs me.

She might think she's the clever one now, but not a bit of it! She's utterly lost without me. But *I'm* fine. I don't need her. Not one *bit* of her.

Well, maybe her hand would come in useful some of the time. So she could do the writing when I get bored.

I do get a little bored sometimes. I go out because I don't want to stay in that smelly old shop, but there aren't many places to go to in this horrible dump. So I just sort of mooch about.

I don't need Garnet to make up games for me. I can make up my own. I mostly pretend I'm this intrepid explorer trekking through the jungle, and there are killer snakes and huge hairy poisonous spiders

and ferocious tigers

and I wade through the rapids

and hang by my fingertips from dangerous mountains

and whenever I get the merest glimpse of the enemy I have to hide because in spite of my superhuman powers and mega-brilliance I am hopelessly outnumbered.

I am planning an ambush when the Blob goes unprotected.

The Intrepid Explorer often starves for days and days. She has to make quick raids into enemy territory

but often has to make do with natural resources.

The Intrepid Explorer did ponder about doing a bit of hunting but she decided she was a vegetarian. Even though she doesn't actually go a bundle on vegetables. Sprouts . . . yuck. Cabbage . . . yuck. Cauliflower . . . double yuck.

If this is a *Memorandum* book, then it's just about *me* . . . and I can jot things down at *random*. I know what that means too, Miss Jeffreys, so ya boo sucks to you. It means there's no plan, and you just shove things in any old how. So these are my random jottings.

I am Ruby Barker and I am a brilliant actress and if my ex-twin hadn't made such a muck of things then I could be starring in a telly serial this summer.

I tried phoning the television people, telling them I was willing to audition for any other part. They thanked me and said they'd get in touch. But they didn't. So I phoned again and they got a bit shirtier this time and said there weren't any parts going spare, sorry and all that but would I quit pestering them please, and if I really wanted to be an actress I needed to get myself an agent and why didn't I go to a good stage school.

Well, how can I go to a good stage school when my rotten old father won't send me to one, though he's sending my sister to the poshest boarding school in the country.

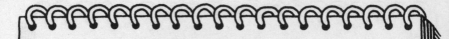

OK, he doesn't have to pay fees, but her uniform is costing a *fortune*.

You should see it too. Talk about awful and old-fashioned! I wouldn't be seen *dead* in those clothes. Garnet looks *appalling*.

Well, I suppose Dad isn't having to pay out of his own pocket. Rose helped Garnet sell her doll at an auction. The crummy china baby doll, twin to mine. I sold mine at the car-boot sale and they gave me £20.

It is exceedingly painful to have to write this next bit. Garnet's doll went for £600. Yes. Mine would have been worth that too. It's some rare French make and daft doll-collectors are willing to fork out a fortune. I mean, you could probably buy a real baby for that sort of money.

Rose was very very angry when she found out the car-boot people only gave me £20. Not angry with me, with them. She went and found them and kicked up a great fuss, but they argued that it had been a perfectly fair deal and she was in the business and she should know they weren't running a kiddie's charity. But they did very reluctantly hand over £100. As a gesture. Rose was still cross because she said they must have made heaps more, but I was happy because that £100 is mine, and although boring old Dad said I should put it in a building society, Rose said she didn't see why I shouldn't have some spending money as I was having a bit of a tough time just lately.

Only I'm not having a tough time at all. Like I said, I'm fine. Doing great. Couldn't be better. *And* I've ended up with £50 to spend all on ME (plus £50 in Dad's boring old building society).

I don't have to waste it on a horrid, hideous

school uniform either. And special suitcases and hockey sticks and dressing gowns and frightful Clarks clodhopper shoes.

I can spend it on

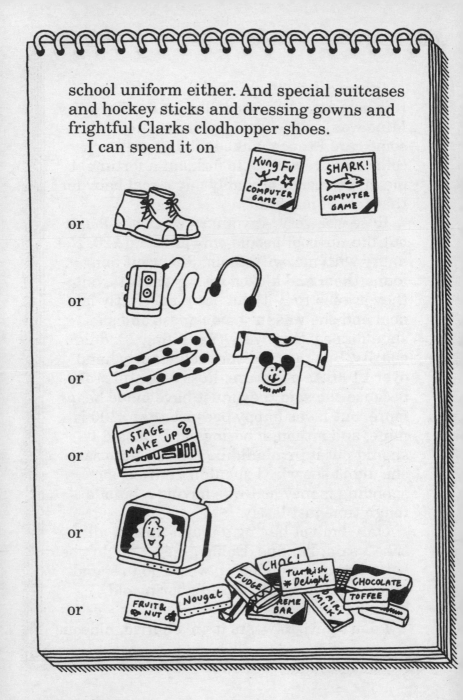

or

or

or

or

or

or

It's weird. I've never had my very own money to spend before. I've always had to share. So it's great to get twice as much.

It's just I can't quite get used to being just me.

I don't even look like me. It's a shock whenever I see myself in the mirror. My hair's growing a bit but it seems to have lost all idea of gravity. It's growing *up*.

This has attracted comments from certain uncouth local loonies, enquiring whether I'm a boy or a girl.

I soon dealt with them.

But then the Huge and Horrible Blob opened his horrendous gob.

He had *such* an inventive and witty new nickname for me.

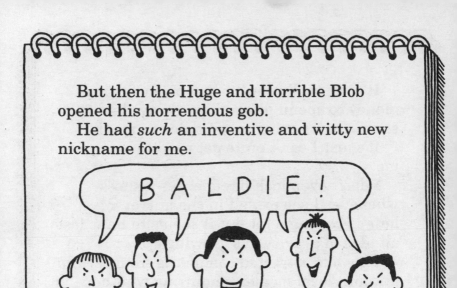

So I invented several new names for him and his stupid mates.

So then they got all these grass cuttings
and asked me if I'd like a green wig and then
they threw them all over me

so I hid behind a hedge until I heard them
coming and then I jumped up and yelled that
they all talked a lot of rubbish so look out—

and they got this black plastic bag full of rubbish all over them.

I'd just grabbed a bag out of someone's dustbin. I hadn't looked inside. It turned out it was wondrously smelly soggy rubbish, all sour milk and tea-leaves and half-eaten Chinese takeaways . . .

So then they got really mad and yelled, 'Let's get her!'

I couldn't run away quite fast enough.

So they got me.

And they smeared rubbish on me and I hit out at them and they kicked me and I bit them but there was only one of me and there were a lot of them.

180

And then while Blob and I were bashing away at each other, this horrible boy with ferret teeth got his arm round my neck and started choking me and I tried to reach round and hit him where it really hurts but he was hurting that wobbly bit where you swallow so much that I couldn't move and Ferret-Face yelled, 'Go on then, Jerry, bash her face in!' and I thought, This is it. I've already lost my hair. Now I'm going to lose my looks. I'm going to have to go round with a broken nose and no teeth for the rest of my days, and it's not going to help my acting career one bit, and I had my face all squeezed up ready for the blow but Blob hesitated.

'Leave go of her, Brian, she's choking,' he said.

'Well, hit her then!'

'Not with you hanging on to her. And all you others. It's not fair. We'll just fight it out, her and me.'

Ferret-Face muttered and moaned, but he did leave go. I reeled a bit, rubbing my sore neck.

'Are you OK?' said Blob.

'Course I am,' I croaked.

'Right. Let's fight,' said Blob.

So he gave me a punch on the shoulder. Quite a soft punch. And I gave him a shove in

181

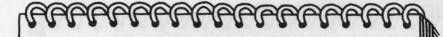

his stomach. But not too hard. And then he wrestled me to the ground. But carefully. And I kicked at him. Though I actually barely touched him. We seemed to have lost interest in a really ferocious fight. We were just sort of going through the motions.

Ferret-Face and the other mates got a bit bored with the whole situation too. And they were fed up being covered in all the stinky guck from the rubbish bag, so they sloped off home.

Blob and I were left.

'Shall we just say that I've won the fight and call it quits?' said Blob.

'You haven't won the rotten fight!' I said indignantly. I gave him another punch, though it was a very feeble one.

'All right all right. Well, how about if we call it a draw?' said Blob.

I thought a bit. And then I nodded.

'OK. Though I could have won, you know,' I insisted.

'You're quite a good fighter. For a girl,' said Blob.

'You're quite a good fighter. For a big fat blob,' I said.

He looked hurt. 'Hey, there's no need to call me names. I stuck up for you! I stopped Brian mangling your neck.'

'Yes, but you call me names. Baldie.'

'Yes, well, you do look a bit bald since you had that wacky haircut.'

'Yes, well, you do look a bit blobby.'

'We *both* look a right sight. Especially now. Covered in all this gunge,' said Blob, wiping bamboo shoots out of his eye.

'You can say that again,' I agreed, picking tea-leaves off my face.

We looked at each other. Then we laughed.

And it's weird. We're not bitter enemies

any more. We're sort of friends.

I sometimes go round in the gang, though I can't stick Brian. Actually, Blob isn't too keen on him either.

So we've started going round together. Just him and me.

He still calls me Baldie.

I still call him Blob.

But it doesn't matter because we're mates.

It's great to have someone to pal round with. Someone different, not someone the same as me.

And both Blob and I are going on to the big school together. I'm glad I'll be shot of that Dumbo Debenham. I'll be a new girl at a new school with new teachers. I could make a whole new start if I wanted. Work a bit.

Well, that's what Dad says.

I'll have to see about that.

But there is one good thing about the new school. They've got a stage. Not quite as posh and elaborate as the one at Marnock Heights, but they've got velvet curtains, and they can put up special lights and rustle up some scenery and they have a proper play in the summer and a pantomime at Christmas. Blob told me, because his sister's been in them.

So I'm going to get to be in them too.

Definitely.

It's all going to be great.

I'm ever so happy.

Garnet isn't happy. She's started crying at nights. She's scared about going to boarding school by herself. But it's not just that. She says she can't bear not being friends with me any more.

I listen. And sometimes my eyes sting a bit, but it's OK in the dark. She can't see.

I open my mouth to say a whole lot of things. But somehow I can't ever get them said into the silence. I can't even manage one word. Sorry.

Well, I don't see why I should say sorry. It's Garnet's fault she's going. She shouldn't have done so well in that stupid entrance exam.

No, she should have tried harder at the audition. Then we'd have got to be the Twins at St Clare's. We'd be acting now. Together.

We've been separate all summer.

It's been a bit strange sometimes.

It's going to be even stranger when she's gone.

It's her last night at home. Rose cooked chicken and chips, Garnet's favourite, and made a cake.

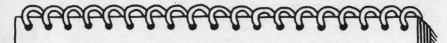

She's never made *me* a special cake.
Garnet could only manage one small slice.
Then we all had to sit around playing daft
games like Snap and Happy Families.
Pretending we were all one Happy Family.
And Garnet looked like she was going to snap.

But she didn't cry. Not even when we went
to bed. At least, I don't think she did. I got
right under the covers so that I couldn't hear.

I felt as if I was snapping. In half.

I kept pretending it wasn't really
happening but then we woke up in the
morning and Garnet got dressed in her
strange new uniform and we've never looked
less like twins in our lives.

Rose came into our bedroom to help Garnet get all her new stuff packed and ready.

I looked at all the new clothes and the pyjamas and the hockey boots and all the other stuff, all exactly my size. But not for me.

And for the first time I was really glad I wasn't going. I knew I'd be scared.

Garnet was so scared she had a funny tummy and had to keep dashing to the loo. One of the times she was missing in the bathroom I picked up her old nightie lying on her pillow and sort of snuggled into it for a second, like a baby with a cuddle blanket.

Rose was bent over Garnet's suitcase but she turned and saw me.

She didn't say anything – but she straightened up and put her arm round me and gave me a quick hug.

I started to wriggle away, but she held on to me. So I found I was kind of hugging her back.

And then I started crying.

'You're the one that never cries. You'll start me off,' Rose whispered.

'Don't be nice to me. I've been so hateful. To Garnet,' I sobbed.

'You haven't been exactly sweetness and light to me, either,' said Rose, laughing shakily. 'Or your dad. But you're right. It's Garnet that really matters.'

It's Garnet that really matters.

My twin. My best friend. My other half.

She came back from the bathroom and I rushed at her, flinging my arms round her neck.

'Oh Garnet, I'm so sorry, I've been such a
pig, I didn't mean it really, I was just so
jealous, and I felt so stupid, and I felt so left
out, but you will still be my twin, won't you,
even though you're off to Marnock Heights?'

'I'll be your twin for ever and ever and
ever,' said Garnet, and we hugged so hard we
seemed like Siamese twins, joined for ever.

Only we were about to be ripped apart.

'It's all my stupid stupid stupid fault,' I
wailed. 'Oh Garnet, I'll miss you so terribly.'

'I'll miss you too, Ruby – ever so ever so
much. But Dad says I don't have to stay if I
really hate it.'

'And you'll come home some weekends –
and all the holidays. Oh, how can I have been
crazy enough to waste all this summer being
so foul? I hate me. Why do I always have to
be the bad twin?'

'Why do I always have to be the good twin?'
said Garnet. 'Hey, maybe we're changing
round. We're starting already. You're crying –
and I'm not!'

'You will still be my best friend, won't you?
You won't go all posh and snooty and look
down on me?' I said.

'Don't talk wet,' said Garnet.

'And you will write to me?'

'Every single day. And you write to me too.'

'I promise.'

'You don't always keep your promises.'

'But this is a promise I'll keep, I swear. And I also promise that I'll never ever be mean to you again, Garnet.'

'You'd better not swear on *that* promise,' said Garnet, laughing.

But she cried a little bit when she and Dad went off in the car. We *all* cried.

Garnet's taken the accounts book with her. She's going to write in it every day and then show it to me when she comes home. I've nearly finished this memorandum book already.

I'll have to get another. Bigger, so I can write more. I'll look and see if there's a Paperchase in Hineford on Saturday. Rose is going to drive me there. She's found out about this Saturday drama club. So I'm joining it.

I was dead chuffed when she told me about it.

'Thanks, Rose,' I said.

Well. It was more of a mumble. But she heard.

'It's OK, Ruby. I'm dying to go to Hineford to see some decent shops. I'll have a lovely time in the shopping centre while you do your drama session and then we'll meet up and have lunch. Yes?'

'You bet,' I said.

She's not quite so bad as I thought, Rose.

It's time I started some serious drama training. For my big moment when the telly people get in touch and ask me to audition. Because they still *might*. If this *Twitty Twins at St Clare's* serial is a success they might want to do another Enid Blyton book. One of the Famous Five stories, maybe. The leading part is this fierce tomboy girl, Georgina. I could play her easy-peasy. I've even got the right haircut now.

When Dad gives me a big cuddle, he ruffles all the bristles and calls me his little

Scrubbing Brush. Dad's needed quite a lot of cuddles. Because he's missing Garnet so much.

We're all missing her.

I'm missing her most.

But she's all right. She sort of likes it.

I'll stick her first postcard on this page.

Dearest Ruby,
          I'm here! At Marnock Heights.
I feel just like one of the girls in those old school books. I cried a bit after Dad left but this lovely big girl put her arm round me. She's called Jamilla and she's my Sheepdog. That doesn't mean she barks at me, she just shows me where everything is, the classrooms and my bedroom and the dining-room. We had chicken and chips for supper. And Jamilla gave me half a Kit Kat. I'm in the bedroom now and there are three other girls and we're all setting our alarms for midnight so we can have our first feast! The girl in the bed next to me is called Lucy, and she wears little glasses and she's got a toy rabbit to take to bed and a real rabbit in the zoo and she says I can share it if I want. She wants to be my best friend and I said yes but you're my bestest best friend, Ruby. x x x
     With lots and lots of love from Garnet x x x x
     P.S. I do miss you so.

Oh, Garnet. I miss you too. Ever so ever so much.

But we're still Ruby and Garnet, even though you're there and I'm here.

We're going to be Ruby and Garnet for ever.

THE END

BAD GIRLS

Jacqueline Wilson

ILLUSTRATED BY NICK SHARRATT

CORGI YEARLING BOOKS

For Rebecca Hillman,
special friend
and fellow writer

RED

Red

They were going to get me.

I saw them the moment I turned the corner. They were halfway down, waiting near the bus stop. Melanie, Sarah and Kim. Kim, the worst one of all.

I didn't know what to do. I took a step forward, my sandal sticking to the pavement.

They were nudging each other. They'd spotted me.

I couldn't see that far, even with my glasses, but I knew Kim would have that great big smile on her face.

I stood still. I looked over my shoulder. Perhaps I could run back to school? I'd hung around for ages already. Maybe they'd locked the playground gates? But perhaps one of the teachers would still be there? I could pretend I had a stomachache or something and then maybe I'd get a lift in their car?

'Look at Mandy! She's going to go rushing back to school. *Baby!*' Kim yelled.

She seemed to have her own magic glasses that let her see right inside my head. She didn't wear ordinary glasses, of course. Girls like Kim never wear glasses or braces on their teeth. They never get fat. They never have a silly haircut. They never wear stupid baby clothes.

If I ran back they'd only run after me. So I went on walking, even though my legs were wobbly. I was getting near enough to see them properly. Kim was smiling all right. They all were.

I tried to think what to do.

Daddy told me to try teasing her back. But you can't tease girls like Kim. There's nothing to tease her about.

Mum said just ignore them and then they'll get tired of teasing.

They hadn't got tired yet.

I was getting nearer and nearer. My sandals were still sticking. I was sticking, too. My dress stuck to my back. My forehead was wet under my fringe.

But I tried very hard to look cool. I tried to stare straight past them. Arthur King was waiting at the bus stop. I stared at him instead. He was reading a book. He was always reading books.

I like reading too. It was a shame Arthur King was a boy. And a bit weird. Otherwise we might have been friends.

I didn't have any proper friends now. I used to have Melanie, but then she got friendly with Sarah. Then Kim decided she'd have them in her gang.

Melanie always said she hated Kim. But now she was her best friend. If Kim wants you as a friend then that's it. You don't argue with her. She can be so scary.

She was right in front of me now. I couldn't stare past her any more. I had to look at her. Her bright black eyes and her glossy hair and her big mouth smiling, showing all her white teeth.

I could even see her when I shut my eyes. It was as if she'd stepped through my glasses, straight into my head. Smiling and smiling.

'She's got her eyes shut. Hey, let's bump into her,' said Kim.

I opened my eyes up quick.

'She's mad,' said Sarah.

'She's playing one of her pretend games,' said Melanie.

They all cracked up laughing.

I couldn't stand it that Melanie had told them all our private games. My eyes started stinging. I blinked hard. I knew I mustn't cry no matter what.

Ignore them, ignore them, ignore them . . .

'She's trying to ignore us!' said Kim triumphantly. 'Did Mumsie-Wumsie tell you to ignore us rude nasty girlies, then?'

There was no point trying to ignore her any more. I couldn't, anyway. She'd stepped straight in front of me. She had Melanie on one side, Sarah on the other. I was surrounded.

I swallowed. Kim went on smiling.

'Where *is* Mumsie, anyway?' she said. 'Not like Mumsie to let little Mandy mince home all by herself. We were looking out for her, weren't we, Mel, weren't we, Sarah?'

They always nudged each other and whispered and giggled when my mum went past. They nudged and whispered and giggled even more when Mum and I were together. One terrible time Mum took hold of my hand and they all saw before I could snatch it away. They went on about it for weeks. Kim made up tales of toddler reins and pushchairs and baby bottles. And a dummy for the dummy.

They were nudging and whispering and giggling now. I didn't answer Kim. I tried to dodge round her but she dodged too, so she was standing in front of me. Right up close. Bigger than me.

'Hey, I'm talking to you! You deaf or something? Had I better shout?' said Kim. She bent so close her silky black hair brushed my cheek. 'WHERE'S MUMSIE?' she bellowed into my ear.

I could feel her voice roaring right through my head, whirling up and down every little squiggle of my brain. I peered round desperately. Arthur King was looking up from his book, staring.

I couldn't stand him seeing. I tried hard to pretend that everything was completely normal.

'My mum's at the dentist's,' I said, acting as if Kim and I were having a completely ordinary conversation.

Melanie and Sarah started sniggering. Kim smiled on steadily.

'Oooh, at the *dentist's*,' she said. She sounded as if she was chatting, too. 'Mmm, yes, well, your mum would have to go to the dentist's, wouldn't she, Mandy?' She waited.

I didn't know whether to say anything or not. I waited, too.

'Your mum jolly well needs to go to the

dentist's,' said Kim. 'She's so wrinkly and grey and ancient I expect all her own teeth are crumbling right away. Gone for a full set of false choppers, has she, Mandy?'

 She smiled sweetly as she said it, baring her own perfect teeth. It felt as if she were biting me with them. Cruel little nips, again and again.

'You shut up about my mum,' I said. I meant it to sound threatening but it came out like I was pleading. Either way it wouldn't make any difference. No-one could ever shut Kim up when she got started. Especially not me.

'Your mum looks older than my grandma,' said Kim. 'No, she looks older than my great-grandma. How old was she when she had you, Mandy? Sixty? Seventy? A hundred?'

'You're just being stupid,' I said. 'My mum's not that old.'

'So how old is she, then?'

'It's none of your business,' I said.

'She's fifty-five,' said Melanie. 'And her dad's even older, he's sixty-two.'

I felt my face flushing deep red. I'd told her when we were best friends and she had sworn she'd never ever tell.

'That's *ancient*!' said Sarah. '*My* mum's only thirty-one.'

y all started miming aged old ladies,
king their lips together and hobbling
-legged.

'Stop it!' I said, and my glasses started to go
smeary. I could still see Arthur King through
them. He'd gone back to his book, but his face
was red, too.

'Oooh, Mumsie's little pet sugar lump is
throwing a wobbly,' said Kim. She stopped
clowning and put her arm round Melanie. 'So
what's Daddy like then? Is he all googly-eyed
and ga-ga?'

'He's got this silly beard and he wears a
smock,' said Melanie, and she looked thrilled
when Kim hugged her gleefully.

'A *smock*! Like a frock? Mandy's dad wears a
frock!' Kim yelled, and they all doubled up
laughing.

'A smock *isn't* a frock,' I gabbled desperately.
'And it's a man's smock, a fisherman's smock;
Daddy just wears it when he's painting.'

'*Daddy!*' They all shrieked again.

My face felt as if it were on fire. I didn't know
how the Daddy had slipped out. I tried so hard
to say Mum and Dad like all the others. I
thought Daddy's smock looked a bit silly too.
And I wished my mum didn't have grey hair
and a big bulky body that strained tight against
her cotton frocks and puffy feet strapped into
sandals. I wished my mum was young and cool

and pretty like all the other mums. I wished my dad was young and strong and swung me around in the air like the other dads.

I wished it so badly that sometimes at night in bed I pretended I was adopted and that one day my real mum and dad would come and take me away. They'd be

ever so young and hip and stylish and they'd let me wear all the latest fashions and play music really loud and eat at McDonald's and they'd let me go round by myself and stay out ever so late and never ever get cross. I'd fall asleep making up all these things about this real mum and dad – I called them by their first names, Kate and Nick, neat, *now* names – and I'd dream about them too, but nearly always, halfway through a dream, when I'd got to the very best bit and Kate and Nick and I were dashing off to Disneyland or checking out the Hard Rock Café, my own mum and dad would suddenly bob up out of nowhere.

They'd generally look even older and more anxious, and they'd be calling for me frantically. I'd pretend not to hear and run off with Kate and Nick, but I'd look back and see them crumpling, starting to cry.

I'd wake up in the morning feeling so guilty that I'd jump straight up when the alarm went and go downstairs to make them a cup of tea, and while they sipped sleepily I'd slide into bed

with them and they'd call me their good little girl. Even though I'm getting big now. And I'm not good, not always. I can be really bad.

'Yes, well, all right, I have to call them Daddy and Mummy because they make me. But they're not my real mum and dad,' someone blurted out. It seemed to be my mouth saying it before I could stop it. It startled me and it startled them too, even Kim.

They stared at me. Arthur King behind them at the bus stop was staring too.

'What are you on about?' said Kim, putting her hands on her hips. Her T-shirt was pulled

tight against her flat stomach.
She was the skinniest girl in
the class, and one of the tallest
too. She said she was going
to be a fashion model when
she was sixteen. Melanie and
Sarah said they were too, but they weren't even
pretty.

I didn't know what I wanted to be when I
grew up. I just wanted to stop being me. I
wanted to grow up a whole new person, not
Mandy White.

'They're not my mum and dad, and my real
name's not Mandy White,' I said. 'It's meant to
be a secret. I was adopted when I was a baby.
I've met my real mum, and she's amazing: she's
a fashion model, she's got this fantastic figure,
she's been in a lot of the papers actually, you'd
know her if I said her name but I'm not allowed,
anyway, she had me very young and it was
going to interfere with her career, so she had
me adopted but she's always regretted it so she
keeps in touch. It upsets my adopted mum and
dad but they can't stop her and she keeps
sending me wonderful presents, all sorts of
clothes and fashionable shoes and stuff, but my
adopted mum doesn't approve and locks them
away in trunks and makes me wear all this
baby stuff . . .' It was getting easier and easier,
the story spinning out of my mouth like silk

thread, and I was embroidering as I went, making it as detailed as possible. They were all listening, all believing me. Sarah's mouth was hanging open and even Kim looked impressed.

I'd forgotten Melanie.

Her head suddenly jerked.

'You liar!' she said. 'That's not true, none of it's true. I've been round to your house, I know your mum and dad, and they're your *real* mum and dad, and there aren't any trunks, and—'

'The trunks are kept up in the loft, see. It *is* true, I swear it is,' I insisted.

'Um, you shouldn't swear on it,' said Melanie. 'Because I *know* it's all a lie. When your mum came round to collect you when you were at my house, she had a cup of coffee with my mum and she went on and on about you, and how she'd had all this yucky fertility treatment for ages and they'd given up all hope of ever having a baby and she said they'd tried to adopt but they were too old but then your mum suddenly started you. "Our little miracle baby."

That's what she said. My mum told me. So you're a *liar*!'

'Liar!' said Kim, but for some strange reason she still looked impressed. Her eyes flickered and I almost dared hope that she'd stop now, that she'd let me go.

I don't know whether I moved or not, edging one half-step sideways. But it was half a step too much.

'Oh, no, you're not going just yet, Mandy Miracle-Babe Loony-Liar,' said Kim.

'Liar,' said Melanie, her head nodding.

'Liar, liar, pants-on-fire,' said Sarah.

They all giggled at the word pants.

'Yeah, what colour pants have you got on today, Mandy?' said Kim, suddenly tugging at my skirt, whipping it up.

'Stop it, stop it,' I said, frantic, clutching it.

But Kim still saw.

'Oh how *sweet*,' she said 'White with little weeny rabbits on! To match the itsy-bitsy bunnies Mumsie knitted on your cardi.' She flicked the rabbits with her long hard fingers.

'Poor Mumsie, knitting and knitting for naughty Miracle-Mandy – when she goes round telling everyone she's adopted! Mumsie's going to be soooooooo upset when she finds out.'

I felt as if she'd flicked a hole right through my stomach.

'How will she find out?' I said hoarsely.

'Well, we'll try asking her. Tomorrow, when she comes to collect you. "How old was Mandy when you adopted her, Mrs White?" I'll say, and she'll say, "Oh, Mandy's my own little girl, dear" and I'll say, "That's not what Mandy says, *she* swears she's adopted",' said Kim, her eyes gleaming.

Melanie and Sarah giggled uncertainly, not sure whether Kim was joking.

I was sure she was deadly serious. I could see her saying it. I could see Mummy's face. I couldn't stand it.

'You're wicked, wicked, wicked!' I shouted and I slapped Kim's face hard.

She was a lot taller than me but my arm reached up of its own accord and my palm caught her cheek. It went bright red, though her other cheek was white. Her eyes went even darker.

'Right,' she said, and she stepped forward.

I knew I was for it now. I shoved Sarah out the way, I dived past Melanie, I dashed out into

212

the road to get away from Kim because I knew she was going to kill me.

There was a big blur of red and a shriek of brakes. I saw the bus. I screamed. And then I fell.

ORANGE

Orange

'Mandy! Oh my goodness! She's dead!'

I opened my eyes.

'No, I'm not,' I said shakily.

Arthur King was bending over me, his glasses lopsided, his mouth lopsided too, gaping open in shock. More people gathered in a ring around me. One woman knelt down beside me. They were all in a fog. I blinked, but everything stayed blurred.

I struggled to sit up.

'No, dear, you must lie still until the ambulance gets here,' said the kneeling woman. 'The bus driver's phoning for one now.'

An ambulance! Was I badly hurt? I twitched my arms and legs. They seemed to move about normally enough. I felt my head to see if there were any bumps. My hand hurt as I lifted it, pain tweaking up to my elbow.

'Just take it easy, dear. Now then, tell me your name and address so we can let your mother know,' said the woman.

'She's Mandy White. She's in my class at school,' said Arthur King.

'Were you one of those wicked children chasing her?' said the woman indignantly. 'I saw! I was right at the front of the bus and I saw them chase her into the road. She could have been killed.'

'I thought she *was* killed,' said Arthur, shivering. 'I should have stopped them.'

'It wasn't you,' I said. I looked up at the woman. 'It wasn't him.'

'It wasn't the boy, it was those girls,' said someone else.

Everyone turned round. But Kim and Melanie and Sarah had gone.

'Tormenting her. And she's only a little kid too! How old are you dearie, eight?'

'I'm ten,' I said. 'Eleven next month, actually.'

'Where do you live, Mandy?' asked the woman.

'Fifty-six Woodside Road. But please, I'm

OK, you don't need to tell my mum. She'd get ever so worried. And she's not at home anyway, she's at the dentist,' I said, trying to sit up again.

I still couldn't see properly. Then I suddenly realized why.

'My glasses!'

'I've got them here, Mandy. But they've snapped in two,' said Arthur. 'Shall I put them in your pocket?'

'How's the little girl?' said the bus driver, steering Arthur King to one side and bending down beside me.

'I'm all right,' I said shakily, worrying about my broken glasses.

'The ambulance should be here any minute. You look OK to me, but you need to get checked over. They'll take you to the hospital and someone will let your mum know.'

'I'll do that,' said the woman, nodding.

'No,' I said, and I burst into tears.

'There, now. It's the shock.'

'I feel like I'm in shock too,' said the bus driver. 'They all suddenly charged into the road, this little one, and then them others, and there was nothing I could do. Lucky job I'd slowed right down because I was nearly at the bus stop. I just bumped her, though. I think she fainted, I don't think she was knocked out.'

'I thought she'd died. She just dropped and

she didn't move,' said Arthur, and his bony fingers felt their way past the kneeling woman and the bus driver and found my hand. 'Don't cry, Mandy. You are really going to be all right, aren't you?' he said.

I couldn't stop crying to say anything and my hand was starting to hurt so much I couldn't even squeeze his fingers. They elbowed him right out of the way when the ambulance came and then I was carried away, even though all I wanted to do was to run home. I tried to stop acting like a big baby, crying like that. I didn't have a hankie and my nose was running horribly right down to my lip, but the kind ambulance woman gave me a tissue and she put her arm round me and told me to cheer up, chicken. She even made clucky hen noises to make me laugh.

Then we got to the hospital and I got scared again because I'd never been in hospital before, and when you see it on television there are always people shouting and covered in blood, and tables where they open you up and there are all your insides glistening in jelly.

Only it wasn't like that a bit. There was just a waiting-room and a lot of people sitting on chairs. I was put

218

in a little cubicle and a nurse came to talk to me because I was on my own. Then a doctor came and prodded me and shone a light in my eyes, and then I was taken to be X-rayed and that didn't hurt a bit though I had to keep still. The radiographer told me how the X-ray machine worked and I asked some more questions and she said I was a clever girl. I was almost starting to enjoy myself. Then I went back to the cubicle to wait for the X-rays to be developed and suddenly I heard Mum calling. Then she came rushing into the cubicle, her face grey, her cheek all puffy from the dentist's injections.

'Oh, Mandy!' she said, and she scooped me into her arms.

It was stupid, but I started crying all over again, and she rocked me as if I was a real baby.

'There, now. It's OK. Mummy's here.'

I burrowed against her soft front and smelt her warm toast-and-talcum smell. I felt so bad about telling Kim and the others that she wasn't my real mum that I cried harder.

'Hang on, poppet. I'm going to get a nurse.

They must give you something to stop the pain. You never make a fuss like this, you're always such a brave girl.'

'No, don't go. I don't need the nurse. It doesn't hurt much, really. Oh Mum, I've broken my glasses! I'm *ever* so sorry.'

Mum didn't mind a bit about my glasses, even though they'd cost a lot of money. 'We ought to be able to Superglue them OK,' she said. 'I wish we could fix your poor old arm as easily! I'm sure it's broken.'

It turned out it wasn't broken at all. I just had a bad sprain, so they bandaged it up and put it in a sling.

'There. All done,' said the nurse, folding up the ends of the sling neatly. 'Don't jump under any more buses, young Mandy.'

I smiled politely but Mum looked fierce.

'She didn't jump, she was pushed,' said Mum.

The nurse wasn't paying proper attention as she rolled bandages. She smiled as if Mum were joking.

'It's not funny,' Mum burst out. 'It's a very serious matter. She could easily have been killed!'

'Mum!' I hissed. She sounded really cross. I'd never heard her be so rude to anyone before.

She put her arm round me to help me, and yet her own arm was shaking.

'Come along, Mandy,' she said, and she whisked me out of the cubicle and down the corridor so fast our shoes squeaked on the polished floor.

There was a bus stop right outside the hospital but Mum got us a taxi instead. I could only remember going in a taxi a couple of times before. If I wasn't so worried I'd have enjoyed sitting back pretending to be posh.

'The little girl been in the wars, has she?' said the taxi driver. 'Kids! When our two were that age we were forever up in the casualty. They keep you hanging around forever, don't they?'

'And when I got there I found my daughter all on her own,' Mum said furiously.

'I had a nurse talk to me before, Mum. I didn't mind,' I said.

'And they didn't even think it sensible to keep her in overnight in case of concussion,' said Mum.

'But the doctor looked in my eyes and checked me all over,' I said.

'Well, as soon as we get home I'm calling out Dr Mansfield and we'll see what he thinks,' said Mum.

She made me go to bed when I got in, though I kept insisting I was perfectly all right. She had to help me get undressed because it was so awkward managing with my arm in a sling – and it was my right arm too, which made me much clumsier trying to manage with my left.

Mum fixed me a special sick-bed tea, on her best black tray patterned with orangey-red poppies. The food was orange too: orange yolk in my boiled egg, orange satsumas, orange shreds in her home-made carrot cake and orange juice to drink.

I scrabbled under my pillow for Olivia Orang-utan. I collect monkeys. I've got twenty-two now. Some are really old and were Mummy's monkeys when she was a little  girl. There's a huge great gorilla almost as big as me that Daddy gave me last Christmas. I like them all, but my favourite is Olivia. She's only as big as my hand and she's very soft and very hairy and very orange.

I tucked her in beside me and fed her some of my orange treat tea. When we were both finished I gave her a little ride in my sling.

'Mind your arm!' said Mum. 'That sling is so you can *rest* it. Don't jiggle it around like that.' She sat down on the side of my bed, looking very serious. 'Now, sweetheart. I want you to tell me exactly what happened.'

My heart started pounding under my

nightie. I clutched Olivia with my good hand. I looked down at the empty dishes on the poppy tray.

'You know what happened, Mum. I ran out in the road. And the bus came. I'm sorry, I know I should have looked first. I won't ever do it again, I swear I won't. Don't be cross.'

'I'm not cross with you, Mandy,' said Mum. 'Now, tell me *why* you ran out into the road.'

But the doorbell went, distracting us. It was Dr Mansfield, who'd just finished his evening surgery. He was nice at first and he admired Olivia and all my other monkeys, and he complimented my bandage and sling too, saying Mum had done a very professional job.

'The nurse at the hospital did it,' I said, and then Dr Mansfield got very irritated with Mum, saying that there was really no point in him examining me if I'd already been treated at the hospital.

I got all knotted up inside while they argued. I slid further and further under the covers, wishing I could snuggle right underneath and play caves with my monkey collection. I didn't want to resurface even after Dr Mansfield went because I knew Mum was going to start asking questions again and I didn't know what to say. So I pretended to be sleepy and said I wanted to have a little nap.

Mum usually thought little naps a good idea

but now she started feeling my forehead and asking if my head was hurting. I sussed that you feel sleepy if you get concussion. I started to worry whether I did have it after all, because I really was starting to get a pain in my head. I got scared and Mum got scared too, though she kept telling me that I'd be fine and I mustn't worry.

Then we heard the car outside and it was Dad back from London. He came running up the stairs when he heard the tone of Mum's voice. He never looks quite like Daddy when he's in his stripy office suit. He always has a shower and changes into his fisherman's smock and baggy old trousers the minute he gets in, and it's as if he's screwed on a new happy-old-Dad face too. But now he forgot all about changing. He sat on my bed while Mum said all this stuff. She started calmly but her voice got higher and higher and when she told how she came back from the dentists to find a woman waiting on her doorstep to tell her I'd been in an accident, she burst into tears.

'Don't, Mum!' I said, starting to cry too. 'I'm sorry. But I'm really all right now, I think my headache's just an ordinary one, and my wrist doesn't hurt at all, so don't cry, *please*.'

Dad put his arms round both of us until we'd both quietened down. Mum went off to make us all a cup of tea, still sniffling. Dad gave me an extra cuddle.

'Just so long as you're safe and sound, poppet. Don't worry about Mum. She's having a bit of bother with her nerves just now, and she's having to have all this horrid root canal work, and now you bump into a bus, old girl! Poor Mum. Poor Mandy.'

He made Olivia wipe my eyes with her soft paws and I was laughing by the time Mum came back to my room with the teatray. I hoped it was all sorted out. But then Mum started on about what the woman had told her, all this stuff about me being chased by these girls, and Dad sat up straight, and I knew there wasn't going to be any more laughing.

'Which girls chased you, Mandy?' said Dad.

'It's those three again, isn't it?' said Mum. 'Melanie and that really nasty big girl and the showy little girl with the curls. I can't understand how Melanie can be so horrid, she seemed such a nice girl, and I really got on well with her mother. I'm going to phone her up and—'

'No! No, you mustn't!' I said.

'Of course we've got to have this out,' said Mum. 'Their mothers need to be told. I should have tackled this right from the start when they turned on you. And we'll have to go to the school too and tell your teacher—'

'*No!* You can't!' I said desperately.

'Now, now, calm down, Mandy. Hey, you're spilling all your tea. Why are you getting in such a state? Have these girls really threatened you? Have they made you keep it all a secret? Are you really scared of them?' Dad asked.

'Of *course* she's scared, the poor little thing. So scared she ran right into the road. Oh dear, when I *think* what could have happened! She could have gone right under the bus and—' Mum was getting tearful again.

'Mandy, you've got to tell us exactly what these girls did,' said Dad.

'They didn't do anything!' I said frantically. 'I wish you wouldn't keep going on about it. And you mustn't tell their mums or anyone at school or else—'

'Or else what, pet?' said Dad.

'They'll all hate me,' I wailed.

'Don't be silly, Mandy, how could anyone ever hate you?' said Mum. 'You're a lovely girl. All your teachers always say you're a pleasure to have in their class. I suppose those girls are just jealous because you always come top and

226

you're obviously well loved and cared for. I know Melanie's mother was very worried that her divorce had badly unsettled Melanie. But still, that's no excuse for bullying, chasing you right out into the road.'

'It *wasn't* Melanie, it was Kim—' I sobbed.

'Ah. Which one is she?' said Dad.

'That big girl – the one who looks much older than her age. I've always thought her a nasty piece of work. I've heard her say some silly things behind *my* back,' said Mum. 'So what was she saying to you this afternoon, Mandy?'

'I – I can't remember.'

'Now then, sweetheart, it's quite important that you try,' said Dad. 'We've really got to get to the bottom of this, even though it's upsetting. She does frighten you, this Kim, doesn't she? Does she ever hit you?'

'No!'

'Are you sure, Mandy? She's so much bigger

than you. And when she was chasing you, are you *certain* she didn't push you?'

'No, she didn't, I swear she didn't,' I said. 'Look, please, I don't want to talk about it.'

I had Mum on one side of me, Dad the other. I felt smothered between them, and there was no getting away, no stopping their questions.

'I know it's upsetting for you, pet, but we've got to know,' said Dad. '*Why* were you running from them?'

'I just – I just wanted to get home.'

'But what were they saying?' said Mum.

'I *said*, I don't remember!' I shouted.

'Mandy?' They were both looking at me, so serious, so sorrowful.

'Come along, Mandy, we've never had any secrets in our family,' said Mum.

'You can tell us anything,' said Dad.

But I couldn't tell.

'I really truly don't remember,' I insisted. 'It's making my head hurt just thinking about it. Please can't I just go to sleep? *Please?*'

So they had to give in. I lay there in my bedroom after they'd tiptoed downstairs. It wasn't anywhere near dark. It wasn't my proper bedtime yet. I wasn't the slightest bit sleepy. I couldn't stop thinking about Kim and Sarah and Melanie. I wished I wasn't Mandy White. I started pretending. OK, I wasn't boring, baby, goody-goody Mandy White any

more. I was . . . Miranda Rainbow. I was cool. I was colourful. I wore loads of make-up and had this ultra hip hairstyle. I wore the most amazing super sexy clothes. I had pierced ears and a stud in my nose. I didn't have a mum. I didn't have a dad. I lived all by myself in this incredible modern flat. Sometimes my friends stayed overnight at my place. I had heaps of friends and they all begged me to be their *best* friend.

I fell asleep being Miranda Rainbow but then Mum woke me up tucking the covers over me and I couldn't get back to sleep for ages. I couldn't stop myself being Mandy White in the middle of the night. I tossed and turned as the quarter-hours chimed, thinking about going to school tomorrow. Thinking about Melanie and Sarah. And Kim . . .

Mum brought me breakfast in bed on the poppy tray. She felt my forehead and looked at my face.

'You still look very peaky and you've got dark circles under your eyes. I think you'd be better off having a quiet day in bed, just to be on the safe side,' said Mum.

For once I was so so glad that my mum was

such a worrier and always fussing. I didn't have to face Kim and Melanie and Sarah. I could stay at home. Safe.

Mum phoned up her work and pretended she was sick.

'It's not really a fib, Mandy,' she said uncomfortably. 'My teeth are still playing up.'

'But you could have gone to work, Mum. I'd be fine by myself,' I said.

'I'd much sooner stay home with you, darling,' said Mum.

Mum didn't like her work much now anyway. She was a company director's secretary, but her company had changed its director and this new one was young and Mum didn't think much of him. She job-shared with another lady, and Mum didn't think much of the afternoon secretary either. She was young, too.

She got in a bit of a state telling me all about them and I got bored, but tried to nod in all the right places. Then Mum tried hard to play with me, but that got a bit boring too. I was glad when she went downstairs to get started on lunch. I tried doing some colouring with my felt-tips but my wrist hurt too much. I got so fed up I tipped the tin up. There were rainbow felt-tips scattered all over the carpet. I got out of bed, sighing, and started picking them all up. Several had rolled right over to the window. I wandered over and stared out, not really focusing through my glued-together glasses. Someone was rocking the pram in the garden over the road.

There were always babies over there. Mrs Williams was a foster mother. But the person at the pram certainly wasn't Mrs Williams. She's big and she wears old Indian clothes. This person was small and startling. I thought she was a grown-up at first. She was wearing very short shorts and a top that showed her tummy, and great clacky high heels. But when I screwed up my eyes to have a proper stare I saw her face wasn't really that old, though she was wearing lots of make-up. She had short sticky-up hair, bright orange, the exact colour of Olivia Orang-utan's fur.

She looked up and saw me staring at her at the window. She crossed her eyes and stuck her tongue out, and then she waved at me. As if we knew each other.

Yellow

There was a phone call for me at teatime.

'A boy!' Mum mouthed, handing the phone over.

I stared at the phone as if it was a wild animal. There was a voice saying something. I held the receiver very gingerly to my ear.

'... so they didn't keep you in hospital long, Mandy? Have you broken anything? Remember when I broke my leg last year and I had that great plaster cast and everyone wrote stuff all over it, even poems, remember that rude one?'

It was only Arthur King. I wasn't really nervous of him.

'I've hurt my wrist, but it's not broken, it's just got a sling. You can't write on it because it's only material.'

'Oh, well. Never mind. I mean, I'm ever so glad you're all right.'

'Mmmm.'

'You're *sure* you're all right? You haven't got concussion, have you? You're not saying very much.'

'You're not giving me a chance,' I said.

Arthur King gave his funny daft-dog laugh, yaaa-yaaa-yaaa, but he still sounded anxious.

'Mandy?'

'Yes?'

'Mmm. Mandy?' he repeated, suddenly tongue-tied.

'What?'

'I feel bad about yesterday. I just stood there. When they were saying all that stuff.'

'Well, they weren't saying it about you.'

'Yes, but I should have rescued you.'

'You what?' I said, snorting with laughter. Arthur King is smaller than me and he's always left till last when people pick teams for Games.

'It wasn't very chivalrous,' said Arthur.

'You what?' I repeated.

'Mandy, don't keep using that horrible uncouth expression,' Mum hissed in the background. 'Who *is* this boy?'

'Arthur's in my class at school,' I said.

'I know I'm in your class at

school,' said Arthur. 'Mandy, I think you *have* got concussion.'

'No, I was just telling my mum who you are, that's all,' I said.

'Your tea's getting cold, Mandy,' said Mum. 'Come along, dear. Say bye bye.'

'I've got to go in a minute, Arthur,' I said.

'Shiver-what?'

'What's that?'

'You said you weren't shivering or something. Yesterday.'

'Chivalrous! Like a knight. Like my namesake, King Arthur. I didn't rescue the damsel in distress, did I? I just stood there and I *was* shivering. Scared. Cowardy custard. Yellow. That was me.'

'It's OK, Arthur. Really. Anyway I'm cowardly, too.'

'Yes, but it's all right for you, because you're a girl.'

'Look, we're not back in those days of all the knights. Girls aren't supposed to be rescued now. They're meant to sort themselves out.'

'But there were three of them and only one of you. I'm a rotten coward. And I'm sorry. Ever so sorry, Mandy.'

'That's quite all right, Arthur,' I said politely. 'I have to get on with my tea now. Bye.'

I felt pleased that Arthur had phoned me. I'd never ever had a boy phone me up before. It felt good. *I* felt good.

But the next morning I insisted I felt really bad.

'I don't feel at all well, Mum,' I said. 'And my wrist *aches*.'

'Oh, darling.' Mum looked at me anxiously. Dad had already left for his work. She didn't have anyone to consult.

'*Please* can I stay at home?'

Mum felt my forehead and looked at me carefully.

'I don't think you've got a temperature. But you do still look a bit peaky. And I don't suppose there's really much point going to school if you can't write properly. All right, then. As it's Friday anyway. But you really will have to go back to school on Monday, Mandy.'

Monday seemed quite a long way away. I could try to forget about it for the moment.

I begged Mum to go back to work. I promised her I'd be fine by myself. I said I'd even stay in bed so she'd know I was absolutely safe. But she wouldn't hear of it. She phoned in sick again.

'Aren't we bad girls?' said Mum. 'Shall we do some baking together, hm? Give Daddy a surprise when he comes home from work. I'll do an iced sponge – chocolate or coffee? You choose, pet. And some fairy cakes? And then how about some gingerbread men?'

I couldn't help much with the sifting and stirring – but my left hand managed the bowl-licking perfectly.

When the cakes and biscuits were all baking, filling the house with warm sweet smells, I left Mum to do the washing up and went upstairs to my bedroom to fetch a book. I peered over at Mrs Williams' house. The pram was in the garden and I could see the baby on its back waving its legs in the air. But there was no sign of the girl with orange hair.

I kept popping back to my bedroom during the morning. The baby was crying one time, but Mrs Williams came out to see to it. She didn't bother rocking it, she just wheeled it indoors. But then just before lunch I saw her! The girl. She was walking down the road towards the house carrying two shopping bags. She was wearing her clacky high heels again, so it was quite hard for her to balance. She was in leggings today and a T-shirt with a man's face. I guessed he was a rock star.

She had a Walkman on and was bobbing her orange head in time to the music in her ears. She even did one or two funny little dance steps in spite of her shoes and the shopping. I smiled – and she suddenly looked up and saw me.

I bobbed back behind the curtain, my heart thudding. I heard the squeak of the Williams' gate and a clack clack clack. I peeped round the curtain. She was still craning up at me. When she saw me looking she waved again. I waved back though I tried to wave my arm in the sling first and then changed to my good arm, feeling silly and clumsy. She started mouthing something. I thought she was singing along to her music, but she was looking straight at me.

I squinted behind my glasses, trying to read her lips. It was no use. I shook my head hopelessly. She dumped the shopping on the path and made opening and pushing gestures. I didn't even get that for a minute, and then I realized. She wanted me to open the window. But I couldn't open the big windows because they were fitted with special locks, so I had to shake my head again.

She sighed with exasperation, her eyebrows raised, and then she picked up her bags and banged on the door with her elbow. She was so skinny I was surprised it didn't hurt.

I spent half the afternoon staring out the window, hoping she might come out again.

'Do stop mooning about, Mandy,' said Mum. 'I've made a nice cup of tea – and we'll try a fairy cake, eh? Come on, cheer up.'

Mum lifted my plaits up either side of my head and pulled. I was supposed to smile.

I shook my head free.

'Mum, can I have my hair cut?'

'Oh, darling, don't be silly. Your hair's lovely.'

'No, it's not. I've got sick of it long. And I don't want plaits any more, *no-one* has plaits nowadays, it just looks stupid. Can't I have my hair short – and sort of sticking up?'

'Like a bird's nest!' said Mum, munching fairy cake.

'Mum, has Mrs Williams got any daughters? Real ones, I mean, not the foster babies.' I started licking the icing off the top of my fairy cake.

'Don't eat it like that, pet. Yes, I think she's got one grown-up daughter in Canada.'

'This girl isn't grown-up.'

'Which girl?'

'At the Williams' house. I saw her yesterday. And today. She was helping with one of the babies and doing the shopping.'

'Maybe she's a granddaughter then. About your age?'

'Older.'

'Still, it would be nice if you had someone to make friends with. Now that Melanie's turned so silly.'

I shivered, wanting to keep the whole scary school world separate.

'Tell you what, Mandy! How about taking some of these cakes over to Mrs Williams? There's far too many for us. And it'll give you the chance to get to know this girl.'

'No, Mum! No. I don't want to,' I said, suddenly desperately shy.

'Don't be so soppy,' said Mum, arranging the cakes carefully on a plate.

'There! Over you go.'

'No, Mum. Please. I'd feel stupid,' I said.

I desperately wanted to get to know the girl and yet I really couldn't just march over and knock on their door. She'd smiled and waved, and yet she'd pulled the face too. She looked as if she could be really really tough if she wanted. Even tougher than Kim.

'You are a funny little poppet,' Mum said fondly. 'Shall I come with you?'

'I don't want to go at all,' I said, and I wouldn't budge.

So Mum went over to see Mrs Williams by herself. I waited in the kitchen, making a pattern in the cake-crumbs. Mum was gone quite a long time. I wished I'd had the courage to go over by myself. Miranda Rainbow would have rushed over the road without a second thought. Why did I always have to be such a silly coward? Cowardy cowardy custard. That was something they called me at school. And Baby. And Polly Pigtails. And Four-Eyes. And Snobby-Swot. Kim invented new names, new games almost every day.

What would she do to me on Monday?

I crammed another fairy cake in my mouth even though I was starting to feel sick. Then I heard the front door. Mum was back, looking a little pink.

'Oh dear, oh dear, that was a bit awkward,' she said. 'Mandy! You silly girl, you didn't tell me what this Tanya was *like.*'

Tanya! A lovely exotic, unusual name. As good as Miranda. No, *better.* It really suited her.

'Tanya,' I said dreamily.

'Do you know, she calls Mrs Williams "Pat" – not even *Aunty* Pat. Though of course she's not related,' said Mum. 'She's a foster child. There was some trouble at the last home she was in. She's meant to be very good with little children so Mrs Williams said she'd take her on for a few weeks. She says she's quite a helpful little thing, considering. But whatever does she *look* like!'

'I think she looks lovely,' I said.

'Oh, Mandy,' said Mum, and she laughed at

me. 'Still, she seemed quite smitten with you too, asking all about you. And she wanted to ask you over to play, but I said you still weren't very well after a nasty accident, and you were having a little lie down.'

'*Mum!*'

'But you said you didn't want to go over there. You insisted!'

'Yes, but – if she *wants* me to . . .'

'Well, I'd really much sooner you didn't. A girl like that! You haven't got anything in common. And she's much older than you anyway. I thought she'd be at least sixteen but she's only just fourteen, can you credit it? The heels she was wearing! I hope Mrs Williams knows what she's taking on.' Mum clucked her teeth.

I crumbled the rest of my fairy cake, wishing and wishing I'd gone over to the Williams' house myself. Tanya would think me a hopeless baby now, after the way Mum had talked about me. I *was* a hopeless baby. Tanya would never really want to make friends with me.

But less than an hour later there was a knock on the door. A jaunty rat-tatta-ta-tat-*tat*.

'I wonder who that is?' said Mum, getting up. I knew!

'Hiya!' said Tanya, as soon as Mum got the door open. She licked her lips as if she was chasing crumbs. 'Thanks for the little cakes,

they were smashing.' She held out the empty plate.

'You haven't eaten them all?' said Mum, startled.

'You bet I have,' said Tanya. 'Well, Simon and Charlie licked the icing off a couple. The baby can't eat cakes because it hasn't got any teeth yet, and poor old Pat is trying to stick to this dopey old diet. So I got lucky, didn't I?' She patted her completely flat stomach and winked. She wasn't looking at Mum now. She was looking past her, at me.

'You're Mandy, right?' she said.

I nodded.

'Let's have a chat, then,' said Tanya, and she marched into the hall in her high heels, neatly dodging Mum's big hip.

Mum turned round, frowning.

'Well, I really think Mandy ought to have a bit of a rest just now,' she said, in her bossiest voice. 'Perhaps another time.' When she uses that voice to me my stomach always squeezes and I do as I'm told.

Tanya just laughed. Not rudely. She had this

beautiful sunny laugh that made you want to smile too. Even Mum.

'But she's *had* a rest, haven't you, Mandy? You want me to come and play with you, don't you?'

She was talking to me as if I was much younger, one of Mrs Williams' toddlers. I didn't care.

I nodded, still unable to say a word.

Tanya was right down the hall beside me now. She put out her hand and touched my arm. She wore purple nail varnish though her nails were bitten right down so that the ends of her fingers bulged. But somehow even they looked glamorous.

'Show us your bedroom, then,' said Tanya, giving me a little push.

I started up the stairs obediently, Tanya following, tapping out a tune on the bannister with her nibbled nails. Mum was left in the hall, the front door still open though it was obvious Tanya was staying.

'Well, just for ten minutes, then,' said Mum reluctantly.

She still hovered uneasily. I was terrified she might come up too. I deliberately didn't look back at her, and when Tanya and I were in my bedroom I shut the door.

'Wow!' said Tanya looking round.

I blinked at her. It sounded as if she actually

liked my room. Melanie had always been very dismissive.

'It's all pink and pretty and girlie,' said Tanya, kicking off her heels and jumping onto my white fluffy rug. She wiggled her toes. 'I've always wanted one of these rugs. How do you keep it so clean, eh? Oh, and I like your *bed*!'

She took a running dive at it, bouncing happily on the pink sprigged duvet, then lying right down, her hair bright on my frilly pillow. 'Mmm, it smells so clean too,' she said, picking the pillow up and sniffing it appreciatively. She dislodged Olivia.

'Hello? Who's this, then?'

I swallowed. 'I have this monkey collection,' I said hoarsely, waving in the direction of the monkey shelf. They were all neatly arranged, paws folded, tails twirling down from the shelf in little loops, apart from Gertrude Gorilla who didn't have a tail and was far too big to sit on the shelf anyway. She sat beside it, her arms out as if she were saying how much she loved me.

Tanya hurtled straight off the bed into Gertrude's hairy arms, using her as an armchair.

'He tickles,' said Tanya.

I decided not to bother explaining that Gertrude was a she. I was getting giddy watching Tanya whizzing round and round my room. I sat shyly on the edge of my bed as if I were the guest.

Tanya still had hold of Olivia.

'This one's still my favourite,' she said.

'She's mine too,' I said, pleased. 'Her name's Olivia.' I blushed, scared Tanya would think me stupid giving my monkeys names.

'Hello, Olivia. Haven't you got a posh name?' said Tanya. She made Olivia's head waggle. 'Oooh yes, I should jolly well say so,' she said, pretending to be Olivia. She had her voice all wrong, but it didn't really matter.

'She's got the same colour hair as me!' said Tanya, and she screwed up her face into a funny monkey expression to match. 'Do you like it this colour, eh, Mandy?'

'I think it's lovely,' I said.

'Of course, it's not *really* this colour. It's sort of mouse naturally. Only that's boring, isn't it?'

'Oh, yes.'

'I thought I might try it black some time. Go all Gothic and witchy. What do you think?'

I didn't know what to say. I was amazed she was asking my opinion. I still couldn't believe she was actually in my bedroom, chatting away to me.

'Or I could go blonde, like you,' said Tanya 'You've got lovely hair.'

'Me?' I said, astonished.

'My little sister's got long hair too. Just like yours. You look like her. I thought just for a minute you were her when I saw you up at the window. Mad, eh?'

I smiled nervously.

'I used to do our Carmel's hair every day. I'm good at long hair. I'll style yours for you, if you like.'

'*Would* you?'

'Sure,' said Tanya.

She sat me down in front of my dressing table and undid my stupid plaits. She brushed out my hair really carefully, not pulling anywhere near as much as Mum does.

'I'm ever so gentle, aren't I?' said Tanya. 'That's because Carmel yells her head off if you tug her tangles. And she wiggles around something awful. You're *much* better behaved than Carmel.'

'Is Carmel at Mrs Williams' too?' I asked.

Tanya stood still. Her face screwed up. I got scared. She went on brushing my hair after a moment, but she didn't answer. I didn't dare try asking her again.

She swept my hair up and wound it round her fingers and then with one deft twiddle turned it into a top knot. She secured it with the bands from my plaits.

'Like it?'

'Oh, wow!' I said.

'And we'll soften it up here at the front,' said Tanya, pulling a wisp over my forehead and doing little curly bits in front of my ears. 'Yeah?'

'Yeah!' I said, trying to say it just the way she did.

I looked so different. Grown up. Almost Miranda Rainbow.

'Got any spray?' said Tanya.

I shook my head.

'You need it, to keep it in place. And you can get all sorts of special slides and bands if you want to wear it up. Carmel used to have heaps.'

Tanya paused. 'I did my little brothers' hair too, cut it once a month and everything. I kept

248

them looking really nice. I've got two little brothers, Sean and Matty. And my Carmel. I looked after them just like I was their mum. That's why they're trying me out at Pat's place. Because I'm good with little kids. But I hoped she'd have girls. Huh! Pat's got little Simon and that gormless Charlie and baby Ricky and they *all* yell and muck around and get messy and play with their willies. I'm sick of little boys. *And* big boys. Me and my boyfriend broke up three weeks ago, and do you know something, it's the best thing that's ever happened to me, because he is a pig.'

She didn't just say he was a pig. She swore and I felt my cheeks go red and I hoped she wouldn't notice. I was ever so glad I'd shut the bedroom door so Mum couldn't hear.

'Yeah, all boys give me the creeps,' Tanya insisted. 'So that's why I thought I'd find a little girl to play with.' She smiled at me kindly. I smiled back, but I couldn't help fidgeting.

'I'm not actually a *little* girl,' I said. 'I'm ten.'

Tanya blinked at me. 'You're never! I thought you were only about eight. Aren't you tiny!'

I blushed even more.

'Still, I'm tiny too. Without my heels,' said Tanya. She saw me looking at them admiringly. 'You can try them on if you want.'

'*Can* I?' I kicked off my slippers and edged my

feet inside the black suede straps. They looked *wonderful*.

The bedroom door suddenly opened and I fell off one shoe in shock.

'Mandy! Watch your ankles,' said Mum, coming in with a tray. She frowned. 'It's not very nice to try on other people's shoes,' she said.

I took the other high heel off, sighing. 'Whatever have you done with your hair?' said Mum.

'Tanya did it. I think it looks fantastic,' I said.

'Hm,' said Mum putting the tray on my bedside table. She looked at Tanya. 'I thought you might like a drink and a snack. Before you go home,' she said. 'Though you'll still be full up with cake.'

'Ooh, no, I'm always starving – even though I stay so skinny,' said Tanya. 'Is that Coke?'

'No, it's Ribena actually,' said Mum. 'And some gingerbread men. Home-made.'

'Gingerbread *folk*,' said Tanya. 'We made them at this home I was in, and it was sexist to call them men, because women wear trousers too, don't they?' She picked up a gingerbread person, examining it carefully. 'We'll make this one definitely a woman, eh, Mandy?' She nibbled along the stumpy legs with her sharp little teeth. 'There, she's wearing leggings now!' Tanya laughed and I laughed too. I took a gingerbread person even though I was far too excited to be hungry. I nibbled as well.

'There, I've got a woman too,' I said, spraying crumbs.

'Don't talk with your mouth full, Mandy,' said Mum. She walked over to my bed, tidying the duvet and pillow. She looked like she might be intending to sit on it herself.

'You can go now, Mum,' I blurted out quickly.

Mum looked surprised and hurt, but she didn't say anything.

She went. My heart started thudding in case I'd hurt her feelings but I couldn't bother about it too much. Not now. With Tanya.

She slurped her Ribena. 'New lipstick, eh, Mandy?' she said, smacking stained lips. 'It'll match my nails a treat.'

She ate her gingerbread woman, and pretended to feed Olivia and Gertrude too, kidding around as if she still thought me a baby. But it didn't matter. Nothing mattered in the whole world because I was friends with Tanya.

She pretended to feed the man's face on her T-shirt too.

'Here, Kurt, you can have a mouthful,' she said.

'Who?'

'You don't know who *Kurt* is?'
Tanya rolled her eyes and sighed.
She reverently stroked his tousled
fringe. 'Only the greatest rock
star ever, and I just love him.'
    'I thought you said all boys
gave you the creeps?' I said
boldly.
    She gave me a little nudge.
    'You're not so shy now, are you?
And anyway, Miss Clever-Clogs,
he's not a boy.'
    'Well, a man, then.'
    'He's not a man either. He's an angel,
because he's dead. Or a devil.'
    'He's dead?' I said, surprised, because he
looked so young.
    'He committed suicide,' said Tanya. She got
up off Gertrude and wandered round my room,
opening the drawers in my play cupboard.
    I didn't mind her fiddling with my things at
all. She got out my big tin of rainbow felt-tips.
    'Wow! Do they all work still?'
    'Yes.'
    'Let's draw, eh? I *love* colouring.'
    I found us both some drawing paper. I took
my arm out of my sling and waggled my fingers.
Yes, I thought I could draw OK. My wrist hurt
but I didn't care. I usually drew at my desk, but
Tanya spread herself full-length on the carpet,

leaning her paper on one of my books. I did the same.

'My mum committed suicide,' said Tanya. She said it so casually I wasn't quite sure I'd heard her properly. I stared at her. Tanya saw I was shocked.

'She topped herself,' she said, thinking I didn't know what suicide meant.

'How . . . awful,' I mumbled.

'Well, she was always a bit zonked out of her brains anyway,' said Tanya. 'It's OK, it was ages and ages ago. I was quite little. Though I can still remember her. I'll draw her, shall I?'

She drew a lovely lady in a long purple dress and she gave her purple wings too, with rows of jade and aqua feathers like frills.

I didn't know what to draw. I didn't want to draw my mum.

'Draw me,' said Tanya.

So I drew her as carefully as

253

I could, trying very hard to make her pretty. I did her short orange hair and her smiley mouth and her little purple nails. I did every strap on her shoes. I even did a portrait of her Kurt on her T-shirt.

'That's good,' said Tanya. 'OK, I'll draw you now.'

She drew a funny, podgy, little girl with lots of long yellow hair. I wasn't sure whether I was pleased or not. She saw me hesitating, so she drew me special strappy high-heeled clunky sandals on my feet. She did a long line of green grass under me. The heels on my shoes didn't quite touch it, so I looked as if I was doing a little dance. She drew a blue line of sky at the top of the page, and then right above my head she did a big yellow sun with rays all round it.

Then she wrote a title at the top. Her writing was rather wobbly and I knew she'd spelled a word wrong but it didn't matter a bit.

MY FREND MANDY. That's what she wrote. And I felt so happy I felt as if there was a real sun above my head and I was dancing in its warm yellow rays.

GREEN

Green

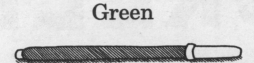

I had to go to school on Monday. Mum took me. She wore her best navy suit though it's really too small for her now. It's got tiny lines called pinstripes. Mum had pinstripes across her forehead too. She only frowns like that when she's very cross.

'Oh, Mum, please, promise you won't say anything,' I begged.

I nearly died when we turned the corner and caught up Melanie and her mother. Melanie went bright red when she saw me. She looked as if she was going to cry.

Melanie's mum started talking to my mum about the weather and the holidays and grown-up stuff like that. Melanie and I shuffled along trying not to look at each other. Then I heard Melanie give a little sniff.

'I thought you might be dead,' she whispered.

I blinked at her.

'When you didn't come to school the next day. And Arthur said you were taken off in the ambulance. But you're all right now?'

'It's just my wrist.' I held my arm out though there was nothing to show. I didn't need the sling any more.

'Oh, Mandy.' Melanie blew upwards with relief, ruffling her fluffy fringe. 'Even Kim was in a right state, I can tell you.'

I giggled nervously.

'Mandy . . .' Melanie struggled. 'Well, I'm glad you're all right.'

I nodded, knowing there were lots of things she wanted to say but couldn't. I felt as if a huge breath was ruffling me all over, making me light and bouncy. I was all right. Melanie was glad I was all right. It looked as if *everything* was going to be all right again now.

But as we got nearer school Melanie stepped aside from me and went quiet. I realized it was in case Kim saw us. And then at the school gate Mum suddenly stopped speaking to Melanie's mum and looked hard at Melanie.

'It's a shame you're not Mandy's friend any more,' said Mum.

Melanie went red again. Melanie's mum looked embarrassed too.

'Yes, I don't know why they've had their little tiff. Still, girls will be girls,' she said uneasily.

'It's more than a little tiff,' said Mum. 'I don't really blame your Melanie. It's that other girl. Kim.'

'Yes, I don't know why Melanie's got so pally with her. I don't see why they can't *all* be friends anyway. But I expect they'll sort it out between themselves,' said Melanie's mum.

'I'm going to make sure things are sorted out,' said Mum, and she marched through the school gate and into the playground.

I dashed after her.

'Mum! Mum, where are you going? What are you doing?'

'I'm going to have a little word with Mrs Edwards,' said Mum.

I felt faint. The headmistress.

'Mum, you *can't* tell Mrs Edwards,' I said, my

voice squeaking with shock. 'They'll all hate me and think I'm a sneaky tell-tale.'

'Don't be silly, darling,' said Mum. 'And you needn't get at all involved. You can go off to your classroom and forget all about it. I just need to let Mrs Edwards know what's happening in her school.'

'But you don't understand, you *can't* . . .' I wailed.

She could. I had no way of stopping her.

I trailed into Mrs Stanley's classroom. Kim was there, standing at the front. She seemed to grow. I seemed to shrink. Melanie was yacking away to her, pointing at me. Sarah was there too, chewing her lip as she listened. I heard the word Mandy. I heard the word Mum.

'Right,' said Kim, and she put her hands on her hips and turned to me.

But Mrs Stanley came bustling in with a basket of roses and started cheerily chatting about her weekend in the country. She sent me off to fill some vases with water for the flowers. I wished there was some way I could stay in the cloakroom all day long, filling vase after vase for a whole field of flowers. But I had to go back and arrange the roses and answer the register and then get out my things for Maths when all the time I was peering out the window to see if Mum had finished seeing Mrs Edwards.

It was halfway through the lesson when I

spotted Mum going across the playground, looking hot and uncomfortable in her tight suit. Her skirt rode up and showed her fat knees. The tightness of her skirt made her walk with a waggle. I saw Kim wiggling her shoulders imitating Mum. Someone giggled.

I bent over my Maths book and pretended to be working, though all the numbers squirmed across the page and my hands were so wet that I smudged the sums I'd already done.

I hoped that it was all over now. But it wasn't all over. It was just beginning.

One of Mrs Edwards' monitors suddenly came into our classroom.

'Excuse me, Mrs Stanley, but Mrs Edwards wants to see Kim Matthews, Melanie Holder and Sarah Newman in her office straight away.' The monitor announced this importantly, so that everyone heard.

All heads swivelled towards Kim and Melanie and Sarah. Sarah started chewing her lip so violently that her mouth went sideways.

Melanie looked like ice cream, white and wet. But Kim looked perfectly composed, though her cheeks were a little pinker than usual. And her eyes brighter. As she looked at me.

I knew what her look meant.

She was really really really going to get me now.

I bent right over my Maths book, clenching everything. I stayed like that long after they'd left the classroom.

I suddenly felt a hand on my shoulder and jumped.

'What's the matter, Mandy?' said Mrs Stanley.

I shook my head, trying to pretend.

'Why are you sitting like that, dear? Have you got a tummyache?'

I nodded.

Mrs Stanley bent closer. 'Do you need to go to the toilet?'

I nodded again.

'Well, why didn't you say so, you silly girl?' said Mrs Stanley. 'Really. You're not a baby, Mandy. Off you go, then.'

I shot off and sat in the dank toilets, crying, wishing I *was* a baby. A little helpless baby who didn't ever have to go to school. One of Mrs Williams' babies in a pram. And then Tanya could still come and play with me.

I sat in the toilets for ages. I read all the rude rhymes, much much ruder than anything Arthur had ever had written on his plaster cast. Then someone came into the toilets calling my name.

'Mandy White, are you in here?'

I hunched up small behind the door, hoping they'd go away.

There was a hammering on the door.

'Are you in there, Mandy? Because Mrs Stanley says if you're really not well you'd better go to the office, and you've got to go to the office *anyway* because Mrs Edwards wants you.'

It was no use. I couldn't stay silent behind the door forever. She'd jump up and look over the top in a minute.

'Just coming,' I mumbled, and flushed the toilet.

I came out and washed my hands. The monitor looked at me curiously.

'What were you *doing* in there?'

I shook my head, not answering.

'Were you sick?'

'No.' Though I was starting to *feel* sick. I looked at myself in the spotted mirror. I was a weird pale greeny colour. A lighter shade of the bottle green cardigan that Mum had knitted for me, even though everyone else had proper shop-bought jumpers.

'Come *on*, then.'

I followed her out of the toilets and along the corridors. I smelt the school dinners cooking in the canteen and felt sicker than ever. Kim and Sarah and Melanie were waiting outside Mrs Edwards' office. I wondered if I was going to throw up all over my carefully-fitted Clarks sandals.

Sarah and Melanie looked as if they felt sick too. Melanie was actually crying. But not Kim.

I didn't dare look at her properly as I scuttled past. I knocked on Mrs Edwards' door and stumbled in. I'd never ever been in her office before. You only got summoned if you'd been very naughty or cheeky or disruptive.

'Ah! Where have you been, Mandy? We've practically had to send out a search party,' said Mrs Edwards.

I hadn't often talked to her in all my years at the school. I'd shaken her hand at Prize Day, and once when I'd done the reading at Assembly she'd smiled at me and said 'Well Done'.

'I was . . .' I didn't like to say the word toilet to her. I just stood there, not finishing my sentence.

'Sit down, then, Mandy. Now. I hear you've been having a rather unhappy time at school recently?'

I sat down and stared hard at my lap. 'I . . . ' I didn't know what to say to this either.

'You've certainly done very well at your lessons, and you've seemed happy and cheerful enough as far as we could see,' said Mrs Edwards briskly.

'Oh, yes,' I said, desperate to agree.

'But for a while now there have been some girls who have been upsetting you?'

I bent lower.

'Some girls in your class?' Mrs Edwards persisted.

My head was nearly touching my clasped hands.

'Mandy! Sit up straight. Now, there's no need to look so worried. We're going to get this little problem all sorted out. If you'd only told your teacher about it earlier then it would have been so much easier to nip this nasty bullying in the bud. So, why don't you tell me all about it?' She waited.

I waited too. Mrs Edwards took her glasses off and rubbed the purple pinch marks on the bridge of her nose. She was trying to be patient.

'Now look, Mandy, there's no need to be frightened. You can tell me. I know it all already, but I just want to hear it from your lips.' She paused. She sighed. She put her glasses back on and peered at me. 'It's Kim and Sarah and Melanie, isn't it?' she said. 'So what have they been saying to you, mmm?'

I couldn't speak. I opened my mouth but no words came out. I couldn't gather together all those worrying weeks of teasing and squeeze them out into short sentences. Especially not with Kim and Sarah and Melanie waiting just the other side of the door.

'Your mother says they've been tormenting you, is that right?' Mrs Edwards persisted. 'And last Wednesday they chased you right out into the road and you were knocked down by a bus? Is that true, Mandy? Because this is very, very serious and it has to be dealt with. Did they chase you, Mandy? *Did* they?'

'Well. Sort of,' I mumbled into my lap.

'Aha!' said Mrs Edwards. 'So what were they saying to you?'

'I – I can't remember,' I said, shaking my head to stop the words echoing in my ears.

'Well, what sort of things do they usually say?' Mrs Edwards demanded.

'I forget,' I said.

Mrs Edwards sighed. She stood up. She suddenly went over to her door, swiftly in her stubby heels, and opened it up. Kim shot backwards, taken by surprise.

'So you've been listening, Kim!' said Mrs Edwards. 'Well, why don't you three girls come in here and join us? Perhaps we'll only start to get somewhere if we all talk this through together.'

They came crowding into the office. I shrank down into my chair. Mrs Edwards shut the door and sat on the edge of her desk frowning at Kim. Kim was taller than her. She had her head stuck in the air, one hand on her hip, acting like she couldn't care less. Melanie and Sarah were shuffling and drooping, much more scared.

'As doubtless you heard for yourself, Mandy here is being incredibly loyal to you girls, refusing to say anything against you,' said Mrs Edwards.

They all looked at me. Melanie blinked at me gratefully. Sarah sniffed.

'But it's obvious to me that you three girls have been very unkind to Mandy and this has got to stop, do you hear? I detest bullying. I won't have it in my school. Now, Kim, Melanie, Sarah, I want you three to say you're sorry to Mandy, and promise that you won't call her any nasty names or chase her ever again.'

They swallowed. Melanie started to say sorry. But Kim interrupted.

'I think Mandy should say sorry to us,' she said, tossing her head.

Even Mrs Edwards was taken aback.

'It was just as much Mandy's fault,' Kim went on smoothly. 'That's what started it. She told us these stories about her mum being a fashion model—'

Mrs Edwards' lips twitched. She was obviously thinking about Mum in her too-tight suit.

'Don't be ridiculous, Kim,' she said crisply. 'Don't make things worse for yourself telling these silly lies.'

'I'm not lying, Mrs Edwards,' said Kim. 'You *did* say that, didn't you, Mandy?'

I bent my head further. I knew I was going very red.

'Mandy?' said Mrs Edwards, her voice wavering.

'It was Mandy who told the lies, Mrs Edwards,' said Sarah.

'And then when we told her we knew she was lying she got really furious and she shouted at us and then she hit me,' said Kim.

'Now really, Kim, you can't expect me to believe that,' said Mrs Edwards. 'Mandy's half your size.'

'But she still hit me. Really hard.'

'She did, Mrs Edwards. She punched Kim straight in the face,' said Sarah.

'Yes, she did,' Melanie said, joining in. 'She hit Kim.'

'And then she ran away and she wasn't looking where she was going so she got hit by the bus,' said Kim. 'It was all *Mandy*, Mrs Edwards.'

Mrs Edwards got up and came and stood beside me. She put her arm round the back of the chair, and bent her head towards me so that her pepperminty breath tickled my cheek.

'You didn't hit Kim, did you, Mandy?' she said softly.

I shut my eyes.

'Just tell the truth, dear,' said Mrs Edwards.

'Yes, I hit her,' I said, and then I burst into tears.

Kim was triumphant. Mrs Edwards looked at me as if I'd let her down.

'I still can't quite believe it of you, Mandy,' she said. But then she frowned at Kim and the others. 'However, I know that you three have certainly been ganging up on Mandy recently. It's got to stop. You're not to call her names or say anything horrid to her, do you understand?'

'Oh yes, Mrs Edwards, we understand,' said Kim. 'We won't say *anything* to Mandy.'

That was the catch. She kept to her word. She didn't say anything at all to me. Neither did Sarah. Neither did Melanie. Kim marched them off and by lunchtime they had their act perfected. They hovered near me, but they didn't speak. They looked at me, they nudged each other, they made faces . . . but they didn't say anything.

I tried to pretend I was Miranda Rainbow, far too cool to care. It wouldn't work though, not with them bobbing about in the background.

Arthur King came over to me, his eyes twitching behind his glasses. He was holding a big old book and he offered it to me like a talisman.

'Here's that book I was telling you about, Mandy,' he said, gabbling a little. 'Do you want to have a look at it?'

Kim screeched with unkind laughter. Sarah and Melanie giggled.

'Over here. Where we can have a bit of peace,' said Arthur, steering me away from them.

The book was *King Arthur and the Knights of the Round Table*. I flipped through it gratefully, my hands shaking as I turned the pages.

Kim and Sarah and Melanie followed.

'Look, clear off,' said Arthur, trying to sound threatening.

'We've got a perfect right to be in this playground, same as you,' said Kim. 'We're not doing anything. And we're not saying anything to *her*.'

She thrust her chin at me, smacking her lips together to show they were sealed. Sarah and Melanie copied.

Mrs Stanley was on playground duty. She walked in our direction. She saw Kim and Sarah and Melanie. But I suppose they looked as if they were smiling at me.

'Let's get away from those loonies,' Arthur muttered, and he pulled me right over to the edge of the playground, by the boys' toilets. Where the girls never go.

We leaned against the wall and looked at Arthur's book together. Kim and Sarah and Melanie kept away, maybe because Mrs Stanley kept walking backwards and forwards across the playground keeping an eye on things.

Arthur kept finding me his favourite bits and reading paragraphs to me. It wasn't really my sort of thing at all. The king and the knights all spoke in this weird old-fashioned way, and I kept getting them all mixed up, but it didn't really matter. I did like the pictures, especially the women with their flowing hair and long swirly dresses. They looked a little like the picture Tanya had drawn of her mother.

My mother came to collect me from school. She wanted to know what Mrs Edwards had said to me, what she had done, how she had dealt with Kim and Melanie and Sarah.

'*Sh*, Mum,' I said, agonized, because we were still at the school gates and anyone could hear us.

Kim and Melanie and Sarah weren't that far behind. They all had their mouths pressed together. Their big new joke.

'Did Mrs Edwards give that Kim a good telling off?' said Mum.

'Mmm. Please, Mum. Don't let's talk about it now,' I hissed.

Mum looked back over her shoulder.

'That's her, isn't it? The tall girl with the black fringe. Well, she doesn't look very sorry. She's got a smirk all over her face,' said Mum. 'Maybe I'd better have a few words with that young madam.'

'Mum, *no*! Please, please, please,' I begged. 'Mrs Edwards sorted it all out and they've promised they won't say anything else.'

'Are you *sure*, Mandy?' said Mum. 'You still look very bothered, darling.'

'I'm not bothered a bit,' I said, trying to smile and act bouncy.

And then I saw Tanya at the end of the road, pushing the baby. Tanya, in her shortest shorts and a tiny top showing off her navel, her high heels clacking at each step.

'Tanya!'

'Hey, Mandy!'

I went charging up the road to greet her. She did that high-five hand thing so I did it too.

'How was school then, eh?' she said.

I pulled a face.

'I get you,' said Tanya. 'It's great for me, eh? I don't have to go because it's nearly the summer holidays. Not that I ever go much. I can't stick school. All them stupid teachers. And silly cows calling you names.'

'They call *you* names?' I said, astonished.

'Yeah, but I call them worse stuff,' said Tanya, grinning. 'Why, anyone giving you hassle, Mandy?'

'Oooh,' I said vaguely.

Kim and Sarah and Melanie were already past Mum, who was puffing in the background. They were staring at Tanya and me. Melanie practically had her mouth hanging open.

Tanya saw me glance at them. She had it all sussed out in a second.

She ignored Sarah and Melanie. They were small fry, beneath her. She looked straight at Kim.

'What you staring at then?'

she said. She wasn't as tall as Kim even in her high heels, but she was older and much much tougher.

'Nothing,' Kim mumbled.

'Good. Well run off home, little girlies. Leave me and my pal Mandy in peace, eh?'

They cleared off. Even Kim. Their faces! Me and my pal Mandy. *I* was Tanya's friend. I was sure they were green with envy.

'I'm taking his Lordship for a walk round the park,' said Tanya. 'Coming?'

I was desperate to go, but when Mum reached us she wouldn't hear of us going there by ourselves.

'No, you can get funny men hanging around there,' said Mum. 'It's no place for young girls on their own.'

'I'll look after your Mandy, don't worry,' said Tanya.

'Thank you, dear, but I really don't think so. Mandy had better come home with me and have her tea,' said Mum.

'Oh, Mum, please, I've *got* to go to the park,' I begged.

'We can have ice creams if she's peckish,' said Tanya, jingling coins in her tiny pocket. 'Mrs Williams gave me some spending money. Oh, please, Mrs White, go on, say yes.'

'No, dear. Perhaps another day,' said Mum, taking hold of my hand.

I pulled it away.

'I want to *today*, Mum. It's not fair. Why do you have to treat me like a baby all the time?' I said.

Mum blinked at me, looking hurt. But she seemed to be wavering.

I was suddenly inspired.

'Mrs Edwards said I should try to be a bit more independent,' I said. 'She thinks I'm too young for my age and that's why the others pick on me.'

'Don't be silly, Mandy,' said Mum, but she sounded uncertain.

Maybe Mrs Edwards really had said something of the sort!

'We'll be back in half an hour,' said Tanya.

Mum sighed. 'All right, all right. If you really want to go to the park, Mandy, we'll walk along with Tanya.'

I took a deep breath.

'No. You don't have to come, Mum. There's not even any main roads or anything. And we'll keep away from any funny men. All the others go up the park by themselves. Not with their *mums*.'

I couldn't believe it was me saying it. Miranda Rainbow had taken over my mouth. And it worked! Mum *let* me go to the park with Tanya, though she didn't look at all happy about it. I knew she'd be hurt and huffy all

evening but for once I didn't care.

Tanya and I ran across the grass, little Ricky jiggling up and down in his pram. Tanya sang old Nirvana songs and I tried to copy her. Ricky burbled a bit too, but then the bumping got a bit much for him.

'Yuck. Baby Ricky's been a bit sicky,' said Tanya.

She mopped him up with a tissue, wrinkling her nose, and then washed her hands in the paddling pool.

'My dad used to take me here when I was little,' I said. 'Sometimes he used to roll up his trouser legs and come in with me.'

'Your dad sounds nice,' said Tanya.

'Mmm. But my mum's a bit . . .' I pulled a face.

I was scared Tanya might tease me about Mum.

'She fusses because she cares about you,' said Tanya, surprisingly. '*I* used to fuss about Carmel heaps.'

'Do you miss her a lot?'

'Yeah,' said Tanya, folding her arms and hunching over. But then she straightened up again. 'Still, I've got you instead now, haven't I, young Mandy?'

'I'm not *young* Mandy,' I protested.

Tanya laughed and pulled my plait.

'You look about six with these.'

'Don't. It's not my fault. I begged my mum to let me have it up the way you did it, but she wouldn't do it.'

'You should learn to fix it yourself,' said Tanya.

We walked up and down slowly, rocking Ricky until he nodded off to sleep. Tanya parked him carefully in the shade.

'But we can do a spot of sunbathing, eh, Mandy?'

She kicked off her sandals and lay back on the grass, pulling up her top even more.

'I've got to get my tummy brown,' she said.

'I don't go brown, I just go pink,' I said, lying down beside her. 'I hate pink. It's my least favourite colour in all the world.'

'Well, we'll just lie in the sun for two

minutes. We don't want you burning,' said Tanya.

I didn't care if I frizzled into a crisp. I wanted to stay lying next to Tanya in the sun forever. I stared up at the green leaves far above us. They rustled, as if they were sharing a secret.

'Oh, Tanya, I'm so happy I've got you for my friend,' I said.

'Ah, you're sweet,' said Tanya. She sat up. 'Hey, you're going pink already. We'd better cool you down. Let's go and buy ice creams.'

We went to the kiosk at the park gates. Tanya bought us a small 99 cone each. Ricky wailed enviously, so Tanya put a little swirl of ice cream on her finger so he could lick it off. He liked this game and moaned for more.

'No, greedy guts. You'll make yourself sick again,' said Tanya. 'Come on, Mandy. We'd better get you home. Can't have your mum fussing.'

We walked along companionably, both of us pushing the pram. Tanya's heels went clack and my Clarks shoes squeaked. Her shadow was bouncy, with fancy hair. Mine was smaller and plodding and plaited.

'Hey, mind Ricky for me while I get Pat her paper,' said Tanya, when we got to the corner shop.

I stood outside, gently rocking Ricky, feeling great to be left in charge of a baby. I peered into the shop to watch Tanya. It was shadowy after the sunlight. I could just make her out, fiddling in her shorts pocket to get the right change for the *Evening Standard*. She handed it over, she took the paper, she walked towards the door.

Then her hand reached out, quick as a wink. She snatched something off a shelf and carried on sauntering straight out of the shop.

'Hey, Mandy. Got you a little present,' said Tanya, holding out her hand.

It was a green, velvet, crinkled hairband.

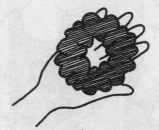

BLUE

Blue

Tanya brushed out my hair when we got back to my house and fixed the green velvet band into place.

'It's called a scrunchie,' said Tanya. 'There! Looks great, eh?'

'Yeah. Great. Thank you ever so much, Tanya,' I said. 'I love my scrunchie.'

My tummy felt as if it was all scrunched up, too. It was so lovely of Tanya to give it to me. She was the best friend in all the world. But she'd *stolen* it.

Well, I didn't know that for certain. It *looked* as if she'd snatched it straight off the shelf. But I hadn't been able to see properly. She might have paid for it with the money in her pocket.

I could ask her straight out. But I didn't dare. It would sound so awful.

'Thanks for my present, Tanya. By the way, did you pay for it or did you steal it?'

And if she *had* stolen it, then what?

I knew it was wrong to steal things. Especially from people like Mr and Mrs Patel, who didn't make very much money out of their corner shop. Although it was only a hairband. A little, velvet, scrunchie hairband that only cost a pound or two. It wasn't as if it was really valuable.

Tanya hadn't stolen it for herself. She'd stolen it for me, because I was her friend. And she didn't have any spare cash of her own. She didn't get proper pocket money every Saturday like me. She had hardly anything at all. So it wasn't really too awful for her to take it, was it?

I felt dizzy with all these conflicting thoughts buzzing round in my head. The scrunchie held my hair up tightly, pulling the little hairs at the nape of my neck. Every time I turned my head it gave me a painful little tweak, so that I couldn't forget about it.

It was almost a relief when Mum made me brush my hair back into its old style after Tanya had gone over the road.

'I know you think you look wonderful, Mandy,' said Mum, snorting. 'But I don't think that style really suits you.'

'I think she looks very grown-up,' said Dad, seeing me drooping.

Mum frowned. 'That's just the point. Mandy's still a little girl. That style's much too sophisticated. And a bit common, if you must know.'

'Still, it was very kind of Tanya to give Mandy that hair thingy,' said Dad.

'Mmm,' said Mum. 'Did she buy it for you specially, Mandy?'

'Yes,' I mumbled. I pretended to yawn. 'I'm ever so sleepy. I think I'll go to bed.'

I just wanted to get away from Mum and Dad. But I couldn't get to sleep. I lay awake fingering the scrunchie. I didn't know if you could buy them everywhere, or just in the corner shop. What if it was a special one – and Mrs Patel realized one was missing from her shelf? What if she'd even seen Tanya take it? What if she saw me wearing the green velvet scrunchie? Did that make me a thief, because I knew it was stolen?

When I eventually got to sleep I dreamt about it. Mrs Patel stopped me in the street and called me a thief. Mr Patel came out of the shop and he called me a thief too. Everyone in the street started staring. There were people from school there. Mrs Stanley and Mrs Edwards shaking their heads and looking very stern. Kim and Melanie and Sarah were standing in a row, chanting 'Thief, thief, thief', their teeth gleaming. And Mum and Dad were there, and they were saying it too, and they were crying, and I was crying too . . .

I woke up in a sweat, still hearing the word thief ringing in my ears. It was the middle of the night now, and the dark made it even more scary. I got up and shoved the scrunchie right at the back of my underwear drawer. Then I lay down again and tried hard to play a pretend game. I was Miranda Rainbow and she never lay awake in a blue funk at nights; she slept soundly in her rainbow sheets, a different colour for every day, and then she got up and had a soak in her jacuzzi and then she got dressed in . . . I tried on various imaginary outfits as if I was a paper doll, and eventually fell asleep again.

I stayed being Miranda Rainbow in my dream and I was still trying on different clothes because I was a famous fashion model now, and I strode up and down the catwalk while the cameras flashed and everything seemed wonderful but then I had to put on this new outfit, a green, velvet, tight dress with a big matching hairband, a huge scrunchie almost like a pull-on hat, and everyone saw me wearing it and suddenly stood up and started yelling 'Thief!'

and I tried to take the scrunchie off but it was too tight, it was tied so tightly round my head I could hardly breathe, it was right over my eyes and blocking my nose and gagging my mouth so that I couldn't even scream . . .

I woke up gasping and sobbing, stuck right down under the bedclothes. I must have made a noise after all because Mum came running.

'Whatever's the matter, darling?'

'I – I just had a horrid dream,' I said, wiping my face with the sheet.

'Hey, don't do that! Let's find you a hankie, you poor little moppet,' said Mum, cuddling me close. 'What was this horrid dream about, eh?'

'I can't remember,' I lied, clinging to Mum. 'But it was just so scary.'

'There. Mummy's here now,' said Mum, rocking me.

She tucked me up tight with Olivia Orang-

Utan and promised me I'd go straight back to sleep and I wouldn't have any more bad dreams.

I tried to believe her. But it didn't work out that way. I was still awake when Dad's alarm went off in the morning.

I felt horrible and headachy at breakfast.

'You and your nightmares,' said Mum. 'Poor old Mandy.' She pulled my plaits fondly.

'Where's the trendy new hairstyle?' said Dad.

Mum frowned at him. 'I think Mandy's seen sense. It's not really suitable.' Mum folded her arms. 'I'm not too sure about this friendship with Tanya, you know. Mandy's started seeing such a lot of her. She's much too old for Mandy. She's a bad influence.'

'What do you mean?' I asked hoarsely.

'Well, you're starting to act really cheeky at times, Mandy. All that business after school yesterday . . . I hate the idea of you going to that park with Tanya. Nowhere's safe nowadays.'

'I think young Tanya can look after herself – *and* our Mandy,' said Dad.

'I'm still not at all keen on them being so friendly. I don't mind Mandy having Tanya over here where I can keep an eye on things, but I don't want them going off together and getting into mischief,' said Mum. 'It's a bit of a risk, a girl with Tanya's background. I've a good mind to stop Mandy seeing her altogether.'

I stiffened. 'No!'

'Oh, come on,' said Dad. 'The girls are good friends. It's great to see Mandy having a bit of fun. And she needs a friend right now, especially after all this bullying business at school.'

That sidetracked Mum.

'Has all that stopped now, Mandy?' she asked. 'Kim doesn't say nasty things to you now?'

'She doesn't say anything now,' I said.

'Well, you keep well out of their way,' said Mum.

I did my best. They didn't hang round near me and whisper things that morning. It looked as if Tanya had scared them off.

She'd been so great to stand up to them like that. She was a truly wonderful friend. And she'd only taken that green hairband as a special present for me. I'd been silly to get so worked up about it. Why did I have to be such a goody-goody baby all the time?

I sat next to Arthur King at lunchtime and then afterwards he tried to teach me how to play chess. It got ever so boring. I wanted to let my mind wander and think about Tanya meeting me from school and how we were going to be friends for ever and ever.

'No, *look*, if you put your queen there I'll be able to take it with my knight,' said Arthur.

I couldn't get worked up about it. The queen

didn't have long hair and a flowing dress, the knight didn't have shining armour and a plume in his helmet. They were just twirly pieces of plastic with no personality whatsoever.

Arthur beat me so easily at chess that it wasn't even fun for him.

'Don't you like chess, Mandy?' he said, setting up the pieces again.

'Not really, no,' I said.

'Maybe you'll like it when you get better at it,' said Arthur. 'I was kind of hoping we could play every lunchtime.'

'Mmm,' I said vaguely.

'And if you're with me then Kim and Melanie and Sarah will keep away,' said Arthur.

'You what?'

'I think I've scared them off,' said Arthur. 'They won't do anything if I'm here to look after you.'

'Oh, Arthur!' I said, too amazed to be tactful. He was the cleverest boy in our class but he was also the dimmest too. 'That's nothing to do with you. It's because of my friend Tanya.'

Arthur looked wounded. 'How can it be this Tanya friend of yours? She's not here. Though it sometimes feels as though she is.'

'What do you mean?'

'Well, you just keep yap yap yapping about her. My friend Tanya says this. My friend Tanya says that. On and on. And it isn't even as if she ever says anything that sounds remotely interesting. It's all make-up and clothes and what-the-stars-say and that rubbish.'

'Are you saying my friend Tanya talks rubbish?' I said indignantly.

'I don't know. I've never talked to her myself. But you just talk rubbish now, when you yack on about her.'

'Well, you can play your silly chess games by your-self, then,' I said, and I slammed down the pocket set with such force that all the remaining pieces jumped out of their holes and bounced on the black and white squares.

I stalked off by myself, though I knew it was a mistake. I wandered the playground for a bit and then I went to the girls' toilets. That was the biggest mistake of all. Kim and Sarah and Melanie were standing in front of the mirror, combing their hair, experimenting with new styles. Kim was brushing her black fringe back, exposing her startlingly white forehead. She caught my eye in the mirror and stopped brushing, her hand frozen in mid-air. Her fringe slowly flicked forward strand by strand until it was back in place.

I should have run for it. But I tried to make out I wasn't afraid. I marched straight past and went into one of the toilets and slammed the door. Then I sat on the loo, my heart thumping crazily.

'There's that girl we don't talk to,' said Kim. 'We don't even say her name, do we?'

'That's right. It's a stupid name anyway,' said Sarah.

'Well, she's a stupid girl,' said Melanie, giggling. '*And* she's a sneaky tell-tale. She went blab-blab-blabbing to her mum and then *she* gets on to *my* mum and I get into trouble. My mum keeps trying to make me be friends with her again.'

'Yuck, friends with *her*,' said Sarah.

'That girl's got a new friend now, though,' said Kim silkily. 'A friend who thinks she's It. Well, she's It, all right. If It equals Filthy Slag.'

That unstoppered my mouth.

'Don't you dare call my friend Tanya a slag!' I shouted from inside the toilet.

They all burst out laughing.

'Did you see the colour of the Filthy Slag's hair? Bright orange. Like she's got a heap of dead goldfish sticking out of her head,' said Kim.

They laughed harder.

'And those high heels she had on! Wibble-wobble, wibble-wobble.'

I heard the three of them stomping about, in crude imitation.

'It's a wonder That Girl's Mumsie lets her go around with the Filthy Slag,' said Melanie.

'Well, they're all mumsies together, aren't they? The Filthy Slag had her little baby slagling in its pram,' said Kim.

'You're talking rubbish!' I shouted, unlocking the toilet door and charging out to confront them. 'That baby isn't *Tanya's*. She just helps look after it. And she's not a slag. She doesn't even go with boys. She can't stick them. So shut up, all of you.' I tried to sound fierce, but my voice was too high, and my eyes were full of tears. Several spilled over and dribbled down my cheeks. They all saw.

'Can you hear a little gnat squeaking?' said Kim.

'What, that little flea that's just come out the toilet?' said Sarah.

'She's a dirty little flea – she didn't even pull the chain,' said Melanie.

I hadn't even used the toilet but they all pulled faces, and Kim held her nose.

I did run then. Crying. And they laughed a lot more.

I kept wanting to cry all afternoon at school. I peered desperately across the room at Arthur, but he wouldn't look at me. I scribbled a little note:

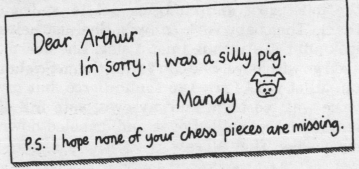

Dear Arthur
I'm sorry. I was a silly pig.
Mandy
P.S. I hope none of your chess pieces are missing.

I folded it up and printed *Arthur King* on the front. I tried to lean past Melanie to get the girl the other side of her to pass it to Arthur. Melanie was too quick. She snatched the note and opened it up and read it. Then she passed it to Kim and Sarah. They were all grinning like anything. Kim wrinkled up her nose and made little snorty pig noises, pointing at me. Melanie and Sarah copied her.

I bent my head over my English exercises. I pressed on my pen so hard I broke the nib and I had to carry on with a blotchy ballpoint. A big tear splashed on the page, making the ink blur. There was another tear, and another, until my page was like a puddle. I felt I was drowning in my own deep blue sea. Kim and Melanie and Sarah snorted and sniggered back in the shallows.

'Who's making that stupid snorting noise?' said Mrs Stanley impatiently.

She looked round at us. I hunched up, scared she'd see my watery eyes. My nose was watery too, and I had to blow it.

'It's only Mandy, Mrs Stanley, blowing her nose,' said Kim.

Melanie and Sarah laughed. Some of the others joined in too.

'Don't be so silly,' said Mrs Stanley, sighing. 'I think I'd better sober you all up. Get out your rough books. We'll have a little spelling test.'

There was a terrible groan. Most of the class looked at me as if it was somehow my fault.

Mrs Stanley called out the words. They looked wrong no matter which way round I put the letters. We had to swap our papers with our next-door neighbour for marking. Melanie. We had to stay work-partners even though she'd stopped being my friend and become my second-worst enemy. Mrs Stanley wasn't the sort of teacher who would ever let you swap seats.

So I had to give my spelling paper to Melanie

and she had to take mine. She just held the very edge of my paper as if it was all dirty and germy, and she threw it quickly down on her desk. Kim and Sarah giggled appreciatively.

I only got twelve out of twenty. Melanie ringed all my mistakes with red pen and made giant crosses. It was my worst ever test. Melanie got fourteen. Kim got eighteen. She came top. She even beat Arthur.

We had to read out our marks to Mrs Stanley. She looked very surprised when I mumbled mine. I thought she might get a bit cross, but she didn't say anything. Then she called me to her desk when the bell rang.

'Is anything the matter, Mandy?' she said.

I shook my head and stared at the floor.

'What happened with your spelling test, hmm? Melanie did mark it properly, didn't she?'

I nodded.

'Are Melanie and Kim and Sarah still saying silly things, Mandy?'

'No, Mrs Stanley,' I said. Well they weren't saying them to me. Just *about* me. But now they didn't say my name I couldn't prove it was me they were talking about. Kim was so clever.

Mrs Stanley didn't look as if she believed me one hundred per cent, but she sighed and said I could go.

Mum was waiting outside, starting to get anxious. But there was no sign of Tanya.

'There you are, Mandy! Why are you so late, darling? The others all came out a good five minutes ago. You didn't get kept in, did you?'

'No, it was just . . . Mrs Stanley was just saying . . . oh, it doesn't matter. Mum, where's Tanya?'

'*What* was Mrs Stanley saying? Never mind Tanya.'

'Just about *spelling*. Boring boring spelling. I thought Tanya was coming to meet me again? She said she was last night.'

'But you're excellent at spelling! You always learn your words perfectly. Look, I thought it would be nice if you and I went into the town and did a bit of shopping. I was in Maxwell's and they've got some lovely pink gingham frocks with smocking on the front—'

'Yuck!'

'Don't talk like that, Mandy! I hate that expression.'

'But I can't go shopping, Mum, I promised I'd see Tanya.'

'Yes, and I told Tanya that you and I were going shopping.'

'Ooooh! But I'd much much much sooner see Tanya,' I said.

Mum's head jerked, as if I'd slapped her face.

My tummy went all squelchy. It wasn't fair. Any girl would sooner have fun with her friend than trail round the shops with her mum.

'Oh well, if you really don't want to, then I suppose I can't force you,' Mum said shakily. 'But you do need some new summer frocks and we haven't had a little jaunt after school for a long time. I thought we'd maybe treat you to an ice cream at the Soda Fountain . . .'

'Couldn't you have asked Tanya to come along too?' I said.

Mum took a deep breath, her nostrils pinched.

'I don't really think that would be a good idea, Mandy,' said Mum. 'You've been seeing more than enough of Tanya recently. Goodness gracious, she's hanging around every day now, the two of you shut up in that bedroom. Daddy and I hardly ever get to see you.'

'That's not true! And anyway—'

'Look, I don't want a silly argument, Mandy. Are we going to go shopping and have a lovely time – or not?'

We went shopping. But we didn't have a lovely time. I absolutely hated the pink dresses in Maxwell's. They were so little-girly it just wasn't true. The size that fitted me was for an eight-year-old anyway. I looked eight in it. No, *younger*.

'But you look lovely, darling,' said Mum,

down on her knees in the changing-room, tweaking the hem and tying the dinky bow at the back. 'We could get you pink and white ribbons to match to wear on your plaits.'

'Yuck!'

'Mandy! How many more times do I have to tell you?'

'Well, it *is* a yucky idea, Mum. I don't want to have my hair in plaits any more, they look stupid. Even Dad thinks so. And *I* look stupid in this silly baby frock.'

'I think you're the one acting like a silly baby,' said Mum. 'Well, all right. You don't have to have the pink frock. Which one did you like? What about the one with the cherries, with the embroidered collar? Shall we try that one on?'

'I don't want a frock at all. No-one wears them any more.'

'I see,' said Mum, meaning she didn't. 'So everyone goes out in just their vest and knickers, is that right?'

'No. Girls wear . . . shorts.'

Mum snorted. 'If you think I'm going to let you wander round wearing shorts like Tanya then you've got another think coming.'

'I don't mean just Tanya,' I said, though I did. 'All the girls in my class wear shorts and jeans and leggings.'

'Yes, well, I don't think you suit that sort of style,' said Mum.

'I *want* to suit it, though. I want to look like the others. That's why they keep picking on me. Because I'm different,' I wailed.

That made Mum waver a bit. So I kept it up. And in the end she bought me a pair of shorts and a T-shirt. Long shorts. *Pink*. But at least they *were* shorts. She bought me a new swimming costume too. Dad and I go swimming every Sunday morning. I begged for a bikini. I thought that way I could wear the bikini top with my shorts. I knew that would look great. But Mum laughed at me.

'A bikini! Honestly, Mandy, you're as straight up and down as an ironing board!'

She bought me a boring little-girl costume. She couldn't pick pink again because they didn't come in that colour. I wanted bright orange but Mum said it was too loud. She chose a blue costume with a silly little white bow at the front and two buttons in the shape of white rabbit heads.

'You look so sweet,' said Mum, trying hard to pretend we were having a lovely time after all.

Mum wasn't even cross when I showed her my broken pen. We went down to Maxwell's stationery department and mum bought me a new ink pen and a matching propelling pencil.

I was desperate to go home right away after the shopping spree but Mum wanted me to have a treat at the Soda Fountain. So we went there and I chose a Cherry Special and I sucked cherries and licked cream and churned the ice cream round and round in the silver dish because somehow it didn't taste right.

Tanya was waiting for me when we got back home at long last. She was perched on the little picket fence round our garden.

Mum sighed as I sped ahead.

'I don't think that fence is really strong enough to sit on, Tanya,' Mum called.

'Yeah, it's not very comfy,' said Tanya, getting up and rubbing the red ridges on her thighs. 'Hey, what're all these carrier bags? Have you been getting presents, Mandy? You lucky thing!'

Oh, how I wished we'd bought Tanya a present! Especially when she'd given me the green hairband.

'Here, we've got you a little present, Tanya,' I said quickly, and I snatched the propelling pencil out of its bag and gave it to her.

Mum raised her eyebrows but she didn't say anything.

'Oh, wow! A present for me! A pencil, oh *great*, I've never had one of these posh propelling ones before. Thanks *ever* so,' said Tanya, and she kissed me. She even reached up and kissed Mum.

'Right – so what have you got, eh?' Tanya said, delving in the bags.

'Oh, they're *lovely*!' she said, holding up my new T-shirt and shorts.

Mum looked surprised but pleased.

'What do you mean, "lovely"?' I muttered to Tanya. 'You wouldn't wear them.'

'Yes, but they'll look great on you,' said Tanya.

'Thanks!' I said, giving her a little push.

'And what else have you got?' said Tanya, rooting in the other bags. 'Oh, a pen like my pencil! And what's this?'

'Just a swimming costume.'

'Let's see. Oh, I like the little bunnies.'

I squinted at her through my glasses, still not sure whether she was acting or not.

'Can you swim then, Mandy?'

'Oh yes, Mandy goes swimming with her father every Sunday,' said Mum, fussing with the clothes, folding them back into their bags. 'Come on, Mandy, indoors. We must get tea.'

'Did your dad teach you to swim, Mandy? Will he teach me? Can I come on Sunday too?'

'Oh, yes!' I said joyfully.

'We'll see,' said Mum.

I knew what 'we'll see' meant. It was a polite way of saying no.

But Dad seemed keen on the idea. 'Yes, of course young Tanya can come along too,' he said.

I whooped triumphantly.

'I'm not sure that's such a good plan,' Mum called from the kitchen. 'That Tanya is starting to tag around after Mandy everywhere.'

'She doesn't tag. I'm the one who tags round after her,' I insisted.

'Now calm down, Mandy,' said Mum, coming into the hall in her apron. 'Goodness, let Daddy change his work clothes and get comfy first before you start pestering him. We'll discuss this swimming later on.'

'There's nothing to discuss, Mum. Dad said *yes*,' I said.

He went on saying yes even though Mum tried hard to make him change his mind.

'I know you seem to have taken such a shine to Tanya – but I'm really worried about her. I've been talking to Mrs Williams and Tanya comes from a really *dreadful* background.'

Mum started whispering to Dad. I tried to hear. I kept waiting for the word thief.

Dad saw me biting my lip.

'Yes, OK, poor old Tanya. It sounds as if she's had a really tough time,' said Dad. 'So shouldn't we try to be extra kind to her, then? Show her what life in a normal loving family is like? She seems a surprisingly nice girl, considering – and very fond of our Mandy. So where's the harm in their friendship? You keep saying Tanya might be a bad influence on Mandy. Have you ever thought that Mandy might be a *good* influence on Tanya?'

I punched the air in triumph. Dad had beaten Mum well and truly.

So we went swimming on Sunday, Dad and Tanya and me. Tanya didn't seem quite so keen on the idea at first. We called for her at half past seven and Mrs Williams said she was still in bed, though she'd called her twice.

Tanya appeared ten minutes later, white-faced and yawning, her orange hair sticking up on end. It was the first time I'd ever seen her without make-up. She looked astonishingly different. Much younger. Softer. More easily hurt.

Dad had been getting irritable hanging about waiting for her, but now he smiled.

'Morning, Tanya!'

'Morning! It feels like it's still the middle of the night,' she said. But she smiled back at Dad. And then she stuck out her tongue at me. 'What are you staring at, eh?' She rubbed her strangely-bare eyes and combed her hair with her fingers. 'I look a sight, don't I?'

'I think you look lovely,' I said.

I thought Tanya would probably have a bikini but when we changed at the baths she put on an old faded navy costume, plain and ordinary.

'I haven't got my own costume. This was Mrs Williams' daughter's school thingy. Isn't it foul? Look, there are all these little holes.' Tanya poked at them with her finger. 'I'm going to get arrested for indecency!'

'It looks fine,' I insisted. '*I'm* the one who looks an idiot.' I tweaked my bow and the stupid bunny heads.

'You look cute,' said Tanya. She sounded wistful. 'You're lucky, your mum doesn't half spoil you. Doesn't she come swimming too?'

I looked at Tanya. We both had a mental image of my mum in a tight bathing costume. We grinned guiltily. 'Perhaps not,' said Tanya.

We stowed our clothes in the same locker. I liked it that my new T-shirt and shorts were curled up with Tanya's top and leggings. I had to leave my glasses behind too. It's always so strange taking them off. The whole world mists over and disappears in the distance. I have to half-feel my way to the swimming pool and all I can see is brilliant, sparkling blue.

'Here, I'll help you,' said Tanya, and she held

my hand tight. 'Where's your dad? Oh, there he is, standing on the edge. Hey, are you going to dive?' She hurried us over to him, our bare feet pattering on the damp tiles. 'Bet you can't dive!' she said.

'Bet I can,' said Dad, just like a schoolboy. And then he dived in and swam away, his arms smoothly dipping through the water, his pointed feet kicking, until I lost him in the turquoise blur.

'Hey, he can! What an old show-off, eh?' said Tanya, laughing at him.

Dad was laughing too when he swam back. He pulled himself up onto the side and sat kicking his legs, little beads of water shining all over him. I was worried about his soft fat tummy and all the hairs on his chest. Grey hairs. But Tanya seemed to think he was some sort of Super-Dad.

'Hey, show *me* how to dive. You're great at it! And I want to swim all smooth like that too, I just splash.' She kept on, but she took ages and ages actually getting into the water herself. Dad had to hold her hands and coax her down the steps. I jumped in. Then even after Tanya was in the water she wouldn't duck down and get her shoulders wet. She stood shivering with her arms wrapped round herself, and when Dad tried to show her how to swim the crawl Tanya wasn't sure she could do it, and remembered she'd had an ear infection and maybe she shouldn't get her head wet.

Dad didn't try and make her do anything. We played bouncing in the water instead, just Dad and me at first, but then we caught hold of Tanya's hands and she bounced too. She shrieked ever so loudly to begin with, but then she started liking it and laughing.

'We're the bouncy family,' she said, as we did a mad ring-a-ring-a-roses. She sang, 'We are the boun-cy fam-i-ly. There's Mandy's dad and Mandy and me.'

We all sang Tanya's song over and over, whirling round in the blue water. 'I wish we really were a proper family,' I said. 'I'd give anything to have you as my sister, Tanya.'

'Yeah, you're like my little sister now,' said Tanya. 'And we'll always stay together and no-one shall ever split us up, right?'

Indigo

School was still horrible. Kim and Melanie and Sarah started holding their noses whenever I went past. Some of the others copied them. Not Arthur. But he was still a bit huffy. I tried not to care. I stalked past with my head in the air, being Miranda Rainbow until Kim stuck her foot out and I tripped.

She didn't try anything when there were any teachers around. Mrs Edwards was stepping up her Anti-Bullying Campaign.

'Wait till the holidays,' Kim said loudly to Melanie. 'Then we'll get her. Round at your place.'

My mum still had this arrangement with Melanie's mum. I went round there every morning in the holidays while Mum worked.

'But I *can't* go to Melanie's now,' I insisted.

'Have they started bullying you again?' said Mum.

'No. Well, not really. They just do silly things sometimes. But don't go back to the school, Mum! I just ignore them like you told me. But I absolutely can't go to Melanie's in the holidays. She hates me. And I hate her, too.'

Mum got very worried. She wanted me to try to make friends with Melanie again.

'But Mandy doesn't *want* to be friends with Melanie,' said Dad. 'And I don't blame her. Melanie's been horrible to her.'

'They used to get on all right. I just don't know what to do otherwise,' said Mum wretchedly. 'I can't take Mandy to the office with me. She's not old enough to be left on her own. But she's *too* old for a child-minder. What on earth are we going to do?'

'It's obvious!' said Dad.

'You mean I should give in my notice?' said Mum.

'No! Have a word with Mrs Williams. I'm sure she'd be happy to keep on eye on Mandy. Then she and Tanya could keep each other company.'

'Oh, yes! *Yes*! YES!' I shouted.

Mum said no. She went on and on saying no.

She tried to find someone else to look after me. But in the end she gave up and fixed it with Mrs Williams after all.

'Oh, Mum, how wonderful!' I said, capering about the room.

'Hey, hey, calm down, you'll knock something over! Now listen to me, Mandy. I want you to behave yourself when you're at Mrs Williams. I'm not having you running wild with Tanya. There are going to be lots of rules, all right?'

'To hear is to obey, O Great Mother,' I said.

We didn't obey any of Mum's rules. Mrs Williams didn't seem to mind much what we did as long as we didn't play music too loudly when the babies were having their naps. She let us go off round the town together and she didn't even get mad if we were late back.

'You are lucky, Tanya,' I said without thinking as we walked into town arm in arm. 'Mrs Williams doesn't ever nag at you and make you stick to rules and tell you off like my mum.'

'Well. That's because she's not my mum,' said Tanya. 'She's just my foster mum. She gets paid for looking after me. It's her job. And she didn't even want me, I was just shoved her way because they couldn't find anywhere else for me. We get on OK, she's not a bad old stick, but she doesn't really care about me. She gets all gooey-eyed over the babies sometimes. I don't know *why* because they're all slurpy and snotty most of the time. But she couldn't care less about me. So she doesn't nag. Your mum nags because she's absolutely dotty about you, anyone can see that. She loves you to bits.'

I didn't know what to say.

'And your dad thinks the world of you too,' said Tanya, more enviously.

'What about your dad, Tanya?' I said.

She'd never really mentioned him.

'Him!' said Tanya, snorting. 'Haven't seen him for donkey's years. Don't want to.'

She unlinked arms and walked on quickly, her sandals clacking. I had to hurry to keep up. She had her face turned away from me. She looked as if she was trying not to cry.

'I'm sorry, Tanya,' I said worriedly.

'What are you sorry for?' she said, sounding fierce.

'Well. I didn't mean to upset you. About your dad.'

'I'm not upset. I don't give a toss about him. Or my mum, not any more. Or even my little brothers, because they've been adopted now and they're doing great. It's just Carmel . . .'

'Won't they let you see her?' I asked.

'We had this supervised visit at Easter but she got all shy and her foster mum was there and . . .' Tanya sniffed. 'Look, shut up, Mandy. I don't want to talk about it, OK?'

'OK,' I said.

'Don't look so down, dopey. Come on, let's get into the town and cheer ourselves up,' said Tanya.

We went into Boots, spending ages at the make-up counters. It was great fun at first. Tanya put all this sample eye shadow and lipstick on me and we squirted ourselves with tester perfume. But then Tanya started sauntering round the shelves – and I saw her hands reach out and grab. She was wearing a hooded sweatshirt with big pockets. It was easy for her to hide stuff.

I followed her, trembling all over. She wandered around, so cool, so casual. An expert.

We walked out the shop and I waited for the hand on her shoulders, the stern voice. But it didn't happen. We walked on, Tanya's eyes sparkling, a grin on her face. She'd cheered up all right.

'Hey Mandy, come on. Better get you to a Ladies. You look a right clown with all that make-up on your face,' said Tanya. She looked at me closely. 'What's up, eh?'

My throat was so dry I couldn't speak. I just stood there, shaking.

'Hey, want to see what I've got for you?' Tanya whispered.

She held open her pocket and showed me a can of hair spray.

'Told you that's what you need to fix your hair. When you put it up. Why don't you ever wear that scrunchie I got you, eh?'

I just shrugged and shook my head. I was so scared of upsetting her again, I didn't dare say anything about her shoplifting.

She started to do it every time we went shopping together. I still didn't dare say anything outright, but I tried my hardest to get her to stay in at Mrs Williams'.

'Please, Tanya. Shopping's boring. Let's stay in and we'll play your tapes or draw or something. Whatever you want. Please,' I begged.

Sometimes it worked. They were the most wonderful mornings ever. We played Tanya's tapes until even I was word perfect. I just mouthed the words though. Tanya sang in her dead-cool husky way, and she did all the right gestures and invented her own special little dances.

'Do you think I'll ever make it as a rock star, Mandy?' Tanya asked, wiggling away.

'You bet you will,' I said.

She dressed up like a rock star too in shiny shorts and a fantastic violet sparkly top that looked wonderful. She painted her lids with purple eyeshadow, doing lovely whirly patterns right up to her eyebrows. One time she took my box of felt-tip pens and designed amazing tattoos for her arms and legs – weird flowers with faces, prancing unicorns, and witches casting spells. She inked a dark purply-blue bracelet round her thin wrist and got me to help her draw a ring on every finger, studded with red rubies, green emeralds, purple amethysts and blue sapphires.

'Do me a tattoo, Tanya,' I pleaded.

'Your mum will create,' said Tanya, but she drew a tiny tattoo inside my wrist. The felt-tip tickled and it felt funny when she pressed on my veins. She drew a red heart outlined with a frill. There were two names entwined, Tanya and Mandy. I felt faint with pride and happiness.

When it was time for Mum to come and collect me I stuck a plaster over my tattoo and pretended I'd scratched myself. Whenever I was on my own I'd take little peeks at the heart. I managed to keep it until bedtime and then Mum made me have a bath. The plaster peeled off and the heart got washed away.

I took my felt-tips with me the next day and demanded another heart. Tanya liked to draw too, using her new propelling pencil. We made up this really great story about two girls who travelled all round the world together. Tanya called her girl Love Tanyanita. I let mine be called Miranda Rainbow.

I was a little worried at first sharing such an important pretend person with Tanya but she took it all seriously and didn't tease at all.

Love and Miranda were poor at first and they had to hitch lifts in lorries and share a sleeping bag at the side of the road, but then Love started singing and had a hit album and made even more money than Madonna. She still stayed best friends with Miranda. They lived in a penthouse flat with white furniture and white carpets and a heart-shaped white bed and a huge swimming pool on the roof with real dolphins and when Love and Miranda travelled the world they now had their own white stretch limousine . . .

Tanya was so good at adding bits to the story that I begged her to write it all down for me so I could remember it all for ever.

'Ther wer to girls,' Tanya wrote, very slowly.

I didn't say a word. But she saw my expression.

'Yeah, well, I'm not that great at writing,' she said. 'I've had learning problems. Because of my mum and stuff. And I'm dyslexic anyway. Know what that is? It's when you can't read and write well. But it doesn't mean you're thick.'

'Of course not,' I said quickly.

'I can't be thick, because I know all the

words, great long ones, some of them. I just don't know how to write them down proper.'

'I could teach you!' I offered.

But it didn't work. I felt too shy to point out all Tanya's mistakes. When I dared tell her something was wrong she went red.

'Hey, this is boring! It's the holidays. Who wants to do school stuff in the holidays? Come on, let's go into the town.'

'No!'

'Oh, come on, Mandy, I'm fed up with staying in.'

'There's not time before my mum comes to collect me.'

'Don't be daft. Your mum doesn't come till half-one. Why don't you want to go shopping, eh?'

'You know why,' I said desperately.

'What?'

'Because . . . because I don't like it when you . . .'

'When I what?'

'You know.'

'No. So *tell* me,' said Tanya, doing up her sandals.

'When you . . . take things.'

Tanya stood up in her heels, her hands on her hips.

'But I always nick something nice for you too,' she said.

'Yes, but . . . I wish you wouldn't. I get so scared.

'Look, it's OK. I know what I'm doing. I won't get caught, honest. I never do.'

'But . . . it's wrong,' I said, nearly in tears.

'*What?*' said Tanya. 'Oh, give me a break.'

'It's stealing.'

'I know it's stealing. But they won't miss it. They mark the prices up to counteract any shoplifters. And how else am I going to get all the stuff I need, eh? Old Pat isn't exactly generous with the pocket money even though she gets paid a fortune for looking after me. It's OK for you to be Miss Goody-Goody. You get heaps of things bought for you.'

'I know. I'm sorry. Don't get mad at me, Tanya. OK. We'll go shopping,' I said tearfully.

'Oh, I've gone off the whole idea now,' said Tanya. 'You've just spoilt it all. I used to get things for Carmel and she was thrilled, she thought I was really great. We used to have such fun together. But you're no fun at all, Mandy White.'

She threw herself down on her bed and hid her face.

'Oh, Tanya, don't, please,' I said, sobbing now.

I couldn't believe everything had gone so terrifyingly wrong in just a few seconds. I could have bitten out my tongue.

Then Mrs Williams knocked at the door and poked her head round.

'Yes, I thought I heard someone crying! What's up, Mandy?'

'Nothing,' I said stupidly, although I was howling.

Mrs Williams looked at the bed.

'Is Tanya throwing a moody?' she said. 'Hey, Tanya?'

Tanya didn't move.

'Never mind,' said Mrs Williams. 'You come downstairs with me, Mandy. We'll have a cup of tea and a biscuit, OK?'

'But what about Tanya?'

'She'll come and join us when she feels like it,' said Mrs Williams.

I was sure she was wrong. I cried so much I couldn't gulp down my tea. Simon came and sat on my foot, staring up at me curiously. Charlie crawled over too, whining irritably himself because he was teething. Great drools ran down his chin. Baby Ricky started whimpering in his pram in the hall.

'Good heavens, you're a moany lot today,' said Mrs Williams. 'So what was the row about with you and Tanya, eh, Mandy?'

'Nothing,' I repeated, blowing my nose.

'Yeah, nothing,' said a familiar voice.

Tanya came clacking into the kitchen.

'I want a cup of tea too, Pat. And let's have

some chocky biscuits too, yeah?' She bent down and tickled Simon's tummy. 'We want chocky bickies, don't we, little pal?'

He giggled and squealed. Charlie clamoured for attention too and she swung him high above her head. He drooled with delight.

'Yuck, you're drenching me, you little waterspout,' said Tanya, putting him down again and wiping her face.

She looked at me.

'Hey, you're spouting too! What's up, Mandy?'

'Oh, Tanya,' I sobbed. 'Will you make friends?'

'We're always friends, you daft banana,' said Tanya, and she dabbed at my face with the dishcloth. 'Here, wipe your eyes.'

'We'll go shopping now,' I said.

'No, it's OK,' said Tanya, nibbling her chocolate biscuit. 'Maybe tomorrow.'

I decided I didn't care what Tanya did. I had to have her as my friend no matter what. Even if it meant she went shoplifting while we were out.

I got terribly scared all the same when the two of us set off for the town the next morning. Tanya looked at me closely.

'Are you all right?'

'Yes!' I said quickly, forcing a smile.

'Come on, tell old Tanya what's bugging you,' she said, tickling me under the chin as if I was Charlie.

'Give over,' I said, laughing too loudly.

I wanted so badly to show her I could be fun.

Tanya might not be that great at reading words but she could read my mood just like that.

'It's OK, Mandy,' she said. 'Look, if it seriously bothers you I promise I won't nick any more stuff for you, OK?'

'Really?' I said, dizzy with relief.

'I'm not saying I won't nick any stuff for *me*, mind you,' said Tanya, grinning. She put her arm round me. 'You still want to be friends with me, yeah?'

'You're the best friend in the whole world,' I said fervently.

We went to the Flowerfields Shopping Centre and at first we had the greatest time ever. We larked around watching the animated mice and bunnies and squirrels dancing through the plastic flower display. Tanya fished out a whole handful of change from the wishing fountain – but then she threw it all back.

'Come on, make lots of wishes, Mandy,' she

said, scattering coins so fast the water plinked.

I wished that Tanya would be my friend forever.

I wished that Kim and Melanie and Sarah would stop teasing me when I went back to school.

I wished that I could turn into Miranda Rainbow.

I wished that wishes always came true.

'What did you wish for, Tanya?' I asked.

Tanya wiggled her nose. 'If I tell then it won't come true,' she said.

We wandered all round Flowerfields. We spent ages in the HMV shop listening to music.

Tanya fingered a new Kurt T-shirt wistfully. I held my breath. But she just gave it a little stroke.

'It's lovely, isn't it?' she said. 'I'll see if Pat will buy it for me. I need new clothes for the summer.'

'I've got some savings, Tanya. I could buy it for you as a present,' I said. I fumbled with my purse. 'I haven't got all my money with me today, Mum won't let me take it all out at once, but I've got nearly twenty pounds at home, honest.'

'You keep it, Mandy,' said Tanya, but she looked touched.

We went up in the glass bubble lift to the top floor. Tanya held my hand as we flew up in the lift together. I was so happy I felt as if we were flying right out in the air, soaring sky high. Then we stepped out into the top arcade and Tanya peered round, sussing out all the best shops.

'Hey, this looks good,' she said, tugging me along with her.

It was a shop called *Indigo*. I'd never been there but I'd heard Melanie going on and on about it. It had a dark blue front with silver slatted doors, the sort you get in a cowboy saloon. It was dark blue inside, with swirly silver lights. We looked strangely blue ourselves and we got the giggles.

All the clothes were on silver racks with special spotlights. They were mostly denim, jeans and shirts and little skirts and jackets, and there were some dark blue knitted sweaters too that Tanya went crazy over. She tried one on and whirled around, stroking its softness.

'I could buy you that instead,' I said.

Tanya wrinkled her eyebrows and showed me the price ticket.

'Wow! Well. I can't afford that,' I said.

'No-one can afford it,' said Tanya, looking at herself in the mirror.

There was a sales assistant across the shop, watching. A fair, good-looking boy dressed in *Indigo* clothes.

Tanya stuck her chest out.

'Honestly, look at that guy giving me the eye,' she said, smirking a little.

'Maybe you're not supposed to try on the jumpers,' I said.

'How can you tell what they look like if you don't try them on,' said Tanya, struggling out of the sweater reluctantly.

She took her time folding it up. I watched her, my heart starting to beat fast. But she put it back on the shelf beside the others.

We went over to look at the jewellery in a case against the wall. We bent over the huge chunky silver bracelets and the rings studded with turquoises. The case was locked so we couldn't try them on.

'Shall I call that guy over, get him to open it for us?' said Tanya.

'No!'

'He's still staring at me.'

She stared back, a silly expression on her face.

'I thought you hated boys,' I said sourly.

'I do,' said Tanya. 'But I can't help it if they fancy me, can I?'

She walked over to a display of cowboy boots, so we were much nearer the fair boy. He had his arms folded, and he kept tossing his head to flick his fair hair out of his eyes. He was certainly still staring at Tanya. He had blue eyes. Dark blue. Indigo, like the shop. He looked the

sort of boy you see in television soaps. The sort
most girls are crazy about. Maybe even Tanya.

'Tanya, come on. We ought to be getting back
soon, because of my mum,' I said sharply.

'We've got bags of time yet,' said Tanya.
'Come on, I want to try some of these cowboy
boots. Aren't they great?'

She bent and undid one clompy sandal. Her
foot wasn't very clean. She stuffed it quickly
into a white studded boot.

'Terrific, eh?' said Tanya, waggling her leg
admiringly. She looked up. 'Oh, oh!' she said.

The fair boy was coming over. Tanya winked
at me and then smiled as the boy approached.

But he didn't smile back.

'Can you get us the other boot,
eh?' said Tanya, her hand
on her hip.

'No, I can't. And you can
take that one off too. You
kids have been messing
about in the shop long
enough. It's time you were
going,' he said.

I felt myself
flushing, nearly
dying of embar-
rassment. Tanya
was red too as
she tried to take

off the boot. She lost her balance and nearly fell over.

'Look, stop clowning about,' said the boy. 'You shouldn't try on boots with bare feet. It's not hygienic.'

He sniffed as Tanya's grubby foot came out of the boot. Tanya said nothing at all. She didn't look at him. She didn't look at me. Her hands were shaking as she strapped her sandal. She turned and started walking out. I scrambled after her.

I saw her hand reach out to a shelf. I saw a blur of dark blue. And then it was gone, but Tanya's sweatshirt was suddenly straining over her stomach.

I tried to make my legs keep on walking. Out of the shop. Along the top arcade. Towards the lift.

But then someone shouted. Tanya turned.

The boy was coming after us.

'Run!' she yelled. *'Run!'*

VIOLET

Violet

We ran. We ran for our lives. There was no time to wait for the lift. We pounded along the upper arcade and then Tanya dived for the escalator. I threw myself after her, hurtling down the moving staircase, barging into cross women, zigzagging past those who wouldn't budge, bumping and jostling so that I banged hard against the rail and for one sickening moment felt I might topple over into thin air, down down down into the wishing well.

I screamed, and Tanya turned. She was already nearly at the bottom of the escalator. She could have carried on running. She'd have probably got clean away.

But she stopped. She started running *up* to me.

'I've got you,' she said, her fingers tight round my wrist.

My head cleared, the lights stopped whirling. I looked round. There were two security guards in blue uniform at the top of the escalator.

'Quick! I'm OK,' I gabbled, and I started running down again, we both did, pushing and shoving and dodging, down until we got to the bottom and they were still only halfway down after us.

'Run, then!' shouted Tanya.

We ran again, and my heart was banging in my chest and I had a stitch and my mouth tasted of metal but I kept on running. I ran as fast as Tanya, who was clopping like crazy in her sandals. The shopping centre was full and though it meant we had to keep pushing we were hidden from view half the time. We were getting near the entrance, skirting the plastic flowers, outrunning the rabbits and squirrels, getting nearer, getting there, getting away.

Tanya suddenly stopped dead. Her fingers

tightened on mine. I saw her staring. I saw what she was staring at. More security men, talking into their radios, spreading out. Waiting for us.

'Quick, into one of the shops,' said Tanya, darting.

But we weren't quite quick enough.

One of them spotted us, and moved fast. We turned and started running back into the centre but we were too late. There was a hand on my shoulder. Two hands, pinning my arms.

'Hang on now, little lady,' said a voice.

'Run, Tanya!' I screamed at her.

But they had her now too, one each side of her, and she was caught, I was caught, everyone was staring and pointing. I heard the word

thief. I shook my head and I struggled and I kept trying to open my eyes up wide, because I so wanted it all to be another nightmare.

It couldn't really be happening.

'Come on now, stop struggling. We've got you. Don't make things worse for yourself. Let's go back to the shop on the top floor, eh?'

'Not her! Not the little one,' Tanya said. 'It's nothing to do with her. She's under age anyway. Let her go. Let her go, you pigs! You've got me, isn't that enough?'

But we were both taken back up in the glass bubble lift, and I couldn't believe that only fifteen minutes ago we'd been so happy and I'd felt we were flying. Now I had men holding me as if I was a criminal. And that's the way people were looking at me, looking at Tanya.

We were walked along the upper arcade and more people were looking and tutting and someone said it was a disgrace, kids running wild nowadays, and they blamed the mothers . . . and I thought about my mum and I started to cry.

'Now then, no need for tears. Don't be frightened, we're not going to hurt you,' said the security man, looking uncomfortable.

'Let her *go*, can't you. She's only a baby,' said Tanya.

'Then what are you doing involving her in your shoplifting, eh? said the man.

'Who says we've been shoplifting? Prove it! We were just having a look round, there's no law against that, is there?' Tanya said furiously. 'And anyway, I keep telling you, the little kid's done nothing. She isn't even *with* me. Let her go home to her mum.'

'You'll get to see your mums after the police have got here,' said the security man.

'I'll get to see my mum, will I?' said Tanya. 'Well, that'll be a surprise.'

They marched us back into *Indigo*. The boy with the blue eyes was standing with his arms folded, shaking his head.

'Yeah, that's them. Stupid kids,' he said.

'You're the one who's the stupid poser,' Tanya yelled. 'We haven't done anything. We were only looking at your crummy stock, trying on the boots and that. We haven't nicked *anything*.'

She went on insisting even when we were taken through to a stockroom at the back. A female security guard came with us and asked us to give her anything we'd taken.

'We haven't taken anything,' Tanya repeated.

I just cried, and Tanya put her arm round me. I could feel she was trembling too, and that made me cry harder.

'Look, kids. Don't make me have to search you,' said the security lady.

'You're not to lay a finger on us! You've got no right. And I keep telling and telling you, we haven't nicked anything. That guy out there, the one who fancies himself, he just wants to get us into trouble,' Tanya insisted.

'He says you took one of their blue hand-knitted sweaters,' said the security lady.

'Then he's a liar,' said Tanya.

But the security lady reached forward and tapped the soft bulge of Tanya's stomach. It slipped. The woman put her hand under Tanya's sweatshirt and pulled. The blue knitted sweater fell out onto the floor.

'Who's the liar?' she said.

'You planted it on me,' said Tanya. 'Didn't she, Mandy? She shoved it at me to frame me, yeah?'

The security men at the door started laughing.

'We've got a right tough little cookie here,' said one. 'I bet when the police come we'll find she's got a lot of previous.'

'The police!' I sobbed.

It was even more scary when they arrived, a man and a woman in dark uniform and police hats.

'Hey, hey! Do I really look so fierce?' said the policeman, laughing. He looked from Tanya to me. 'A little Thelma and Louise, eh?'

'Oh, ha ha. A comedian,' said Tanya.

'Well, you're the hard nut,' said the policeman. He walked towards me. I cowered away from him, snivelling. 'So who's this little shrinking violet, eh?'

'Give over, you're frightening her,' said the policewoman putting her arm round me. 'Don't cry, now. What's your name, eh?'

'Mandy,' I wept.

'And how old are you, Mandy?'

'Ten.'

'She's got nothing to do with this. She's just a little kid who tagged after me,' said Tanya fiercely. 'Let her go.'

The policewoman patted me gently. 'Well, we're certainly not in the habit of taking prisoners as little as you, poppet.'

Tanya hunched herself up small. 'Couldn't you let us both go, please?' she asked, sniffing.

'She's a great little actress,' said the security woman.

But the policewoman seemed to be on our side.

'As both the girls are so young and your property has been recovered, do you still want to go ahead and have us prosecute, sir?' said the policewoman to the boy with the blue eyes.

Tanya and I stared at him pleadingly.

'It's strict *Indigo* policy. Shoplifters are always prosecuted,' he said, folding his arms. 'Half the time it's kids like these two. They're a pest. They need to be taught a lesson.'

'In that case, sir, you'd better come with us to the station and make a full statement there,' said the policeman. 'Now, you say you saw the older girl take the sweater?'

'It's hand-knitted. Sells at £95,' said the boy indignantly.

'You've got expensive taste, young lady,' said the policeman to Tanya. He turned to the security woman. 'And she had this sweater on her when you stopped her?'

'It was stuffed up her own sweatshirt. I could see this little blue cuff hanging down, so I pulled.'

'She should have waited till you lot came before searching me, shouldn't she?' said Tanya. 'You've got no real proof now, have you?'

'We've got proof all right,' said the boy with the blue eyes. 'We've got video cameras installed. We'll have a lovely little film of you stealing our sweater.'

Tanya saw he wasn't fooling. She still didn't give up on my account.

'Then your precious film will show that this little kid here didn't do anything,' she said, pointing to me.

'She was larking around with you. And then she ran off when you did,' said the boy.

'That's not a crime, is it?' said Tanya. 'She's not a thief.'

'But I'm afraid we've got reasonable grounds to think you're a thief, young woman,' said the policeman. 'So I'm therefore arresting you.'

I listened to him cautioning her, the words so familiar from all the police series on the television – and I still couldn't believe it was really happening.

'We're really being arrested!' I whispered.

'We're not arresting you, pet,' said the policewoman. 'You'd better come along to the police station with your friend, and tell us exactly what happened, then we'll get your mum to come and take you home, OK?'

'But you're arresting Tanya?'

'I'm afraid so,' she said.

We had to walk all the way back out of the shopping centre, the policewoman holding me, the policeman holding Tanya. She tried to wriggle and dodge once or twice, but he held her firmly by the shoulders and just laughed at her.

There was a white police patrol car at the back of the shopping centre. More people stared as Tanya and I were put in the back, the policewoman in between us. I was still crying.

'Let me sit next to Mandy,' said Tanya.

'Sorry, love,' said the policewoman.

'But she needs me to hold her,' said Tanya.

'Yes, I know. But you could try and pass something to her, couldn't you?'

'Look.' Tanya waggled her empty hand in front of the policewoman's face. 'See? Empty. So can I at least hold her hand?'

'All right then.'

So we drove to the police station with Tanya holding my hand tight across the policewoman's lap. And all the time her small strong fingers with their bitten nails were clinging to me I felt just a tiny bit braver.

'You could have run off and left me,' I said. 'But you stayed. So I wouldn't be scared on my own.'

'Yeah. Daft, wasn't I?' said Tanya, and she grinned at me.

I saw her looking at the lock in the back of

the car. The policewoman saw her looking too.

'Kiddielocks,' she said. 'So don't try to jump out, pal.'

'Foiled again,' said Tanya, tutting.

She was acting daft, as if it didn't really matter. I knew why. It was to try to make it easier for me. All I could do was grip her hand in gratitude.

Then we got to the police station and even Tanya couldn't grin and act the fool. We were taken across a yard and through a security door and down a dark corridor and into a big room with a desk and a bench.

'The Custody Suite,' said Tanya, looking round.

'Sounds like you've been in one or two already?' said the policewoman.

Tanya gave her a tiny tired smile and sat down heavily on the bench. I sat beside her, huddling up to her.

'Sit further apart, girls,' said a new policeman. 'Now, I'm Sergeant Stockton. I want you both to tell me your names and addresses and then I'll give your parents a ring.'

'What's your mum going to say, Mandy?' said Tanya. 'She'll kill me.'

'What about your own mum?' said Sergeant Stockton sternly.

'Haven't got one,' said Tanya. 'Haven't got a dad either now. He's not considered a fit parent, right? So you want my appropriate adult, yeah?'

The sergeant nodded. 'That's the ticket. Sounds like you could fill in this form quicker than me, young lady. So who is it to be?'

'Well, you'd better phone Pat, my foster mum. She'll be going spare anyway, wondering why we're not back. Now look, Sergeant Stockton. I've got to make something clear.' Tanya got off the bench and went over and stood by his desk. 'I'm going to be absolutely honest.'

'That's right. Make my day,' said the Sergeant.

'No, I'm not messing about. I'm being serious. The little kid over there—'

'You say she's nothing to do with you?'

'Well, she is. Obviously. But she's just the kid over the road. She's looked after by my foster mum while her mum works mornings. She tags round after me. We do go round together. But I swear to you, she's never nicked a thing. She's a real little goody-goody and she comes from a lovely family and she's never ever been in any trouble before. She's only here because of me. So you'll let her go, won't you? You won't even caution her?'

The sergeant smiled at Tanya. 'It's OK. She just needed to be taken to a place of safety. But she can go home as soon as her mum comes.'

'What about Tanya?' I asked. 'Will she be able to go home too?'

'Eventually,' said the sergeant.

'What does that mean?' said Tanya. But it looked as if she knew. She came back and  slumped on the bench. She shut her eyes as if she was trying not to cry. This time she wasn't pretending.

I got closer and put my arm round her. The sergeant frowned a little, but let us sit close this time. I held Tanya all the time the sergeant filled out his custody record. She gave all mad made-up answers at first, but she knew that Mrs Williams would be here soon, so she changed her mind and told the truth.

'And now you've got my name and date of birth you can tap into your computer and find out my vast criminal record, eh?' said Tanya.

'Technology at our fingertips,' said the sergeant.

'Juvenile court, here I come,' said Tanya.

'Is that like prison?' I whispered, terrified. 'They won't lock you up, will they? Oh Tanya, I can't stand it if they take you away. I've *got* to keep seeing you.'

'Get real, Mandy,' said Tanya, her shoulders tense under my arm. 'Your mum isn't going to let you come near me now, no matter what.'

Mum was white and shaking when she arrived. Mrs Williams was with her, with the three little boys, all of them whimpering. Tanya sighed deeply. She looked at Mrs Williams. She looked at Mum.

'Sorry,' she said. It came out wrong. I knew she really truly meant it, but it sounded as if she was being cheeky and defiant.

'It's a bit late for saying sorry,' said Mrs Williams.

My mum didn't say anything. But I saw the way she looked at Tanya. I knew Tanya was right.

I started crying again then, because I couldn't bear it. Mum and I were taken to this other room and an inspector came to talk to us.

'You've been a very silly girl, Mandy,' he said solemnly. 'I hope you've learnt your lesson now. You mustn't ever go round with anyone who shoplifts. They'll get into trouble and they'll get *you* into trouble too.'

Then he started talking to Mum – and he treated her as if she was a silly girl too.

'I really feel it's not sensible to let a little girl like Mandy trot round with a tough teenager like Tanya,' he said. 'My advice would be to keep a proper eye on Mandy in future and maybe vet her friends more thoroughly.'

Mum swallowed painfully, bright pink now. She cried too on the way home.

'I can't believe this is happening,' she said, over and over. She kept looking at me and shaking her head and collapsing into fresh tears.

She phoned Dad when we got home and he left the office straightaway. I had the two of them talking to me all afternoon. Saying the same things over and over again. Saying how sad and sorry they were. Saying they felt so ashamed. Saying they couldn't believe how I'd deceived them, going off on these shopping trips with Tanya. Saying they couldn't bear it that I hadn't told them about Tanya's shoplifting.

Then they started getting cross with each other as well as with me.

'I said over and over again that I didn't want Mandy mixed up with that Tanya,' said Mum. 'But you wouldn't listen to me. You thought you knew best. And now look what's happened!'

'All right, all right.

There's no need to rub it in. I didn't dream it would come to this. I always thought Mandy had enough sense to stick to what she knew was right. If you didn't baby her quite so much then maybe she'd be able to stand up for herself better,' said Dad.

I cried harder and they stopped shouting and Mum mopped my face and Dad got me a drink of water and then they both gave me a cuddle.

'We're terribly upset and disappointed – but we do realize it wasn't all your fault, darling. Don't cry so,' said Mum.

'Come on, little Polly Pigtails, stop the tears. It's all over now,' said Dad.

'But what about *Tanya*?' I sobbed.

'Never mind about Tanya!' said Mum.

'You'll find another friend soon, Mandy,' said Dad.

'But Tanya's my best ever friend! I can still see her, can't I? She won't ever go shoplifting again. She promised she wouldn't anyway, it was just because that boy in *Indigo* was so horrid. But it won't happen again. She hated getting me into trouble too. She tried so hard to get me off. She could have run away and left me but she didn't, she stayed to look after me. Oh, please, you've *got* to understand. I just *have* to see her.'

I kept rushing to the window, waiting for Tanya to come back. A car pulled up outside the

Williams' house late in the afternoon. There was a young woman driving, Mrs Williams and the three boys – and Tanya.

I felt weak with relief. At least they hadn't locked her up somewhere. But she looked awful when she got out the car. She wasn't walking with her usual bounce. Her hair was sticking up on end as if she'd been running her fingers through it.

'I've *got* to see what they're going to do to her,' I said.

But they wouldn't let me. Mum went to see Mrs Williams instead. Mum was very angry with her, because she felt she shouldn't have let me go out round the town with Tanya. I waited desperately for her to come back. Mum was gone quite a while. And when she came back she looked strange. Startled.

'What is it, Mum? What's going to happen to Tanya? Has she got to go to court?'

Mum nodded. 'Thank goodness you're not going to be involved at all, Mandy.'

'I thought they'd just caution her,' said Dad.

'Apparently she's had lots of cautions already. They're going to take a full case history and take all her background into consideration. It's likely to take weeks,' said Mum.

'So she'll be home here for weeks?' I said.

Mum put her arm round me. 'No, dear,

Tanya isn't going to be here,' she said. 'She's going to go to a children's home. Pat Williams feels she can't cope. I can see she's got a point. She was talked into fostering Tanya and she always made it plain she'd have to go if there was any trouble. I mean, she's got those little boys to think about.'

'So she's just washing her hands of Tanya?' said Dad, sounding shocked.

'What else can she do?' said Mum.

'If I'd stolen that jumper would you get rid of me?' I said.

'Don't be so silly, Mandy.'

'But *would* you?'

'No, of course not. You know we wouldn't. We love you and we'll go on loving you no matter what you do,' said Mum.

'But no-one loves poor old Tanya,' said Dad.

'*I* love her!' I said. 'When has she got to go?'

'Well, right now,' said Mum. 'It does seem a bit . . . but I suppose there's no point dragging these things out. Her social worker's there now, helping her get her bag packed.'

'She's going *now*?' I said. 'Then I've got to say goodbye to her.'

'No, you're not going near her,' said Mum.

'It's maybe not a good idea, Mandy,' said Dad.

'I'll just say goodbye,' I said. 'I've got to. You can't stop me.'

There was a pile of my things on the living room table, puzzles and books and my big tin of felt-tips. I peered at them desperately and then grabbed the rainbow pens. I was out of the living room, down the hall and out the front door before Mum and Dad realized what was happening.

Dad caught me up as I was hammering on Mrs Williams' door. 'Now, Mandy, come on, come back home,' he said.

Mrs Williams answered the door and stared at us.

'Is Tanya really going?' I said.

Mrs Williams nodded, looking dazed.

'It's for the best,' she said, though she didn't look certain.

'Can I say goodbye?' I begged.

Mrs Williams looked at Dad.

'Oh, all right,' said Dad. 'Go on, be quick. I'll wait here.'

I went charging up the stairs and into Tanya's bedroom. The social worker lady was there, scooping Tanya's stuff into a big plastic bag. Tanya was sitting on her bed, not helping.

'Hi, Mandy,' said Tanya flatly.

'Oh, Tanya!' I said, rushing to her. 'You're going?'

Her fists were clenched. Her face looked clenched too.

'Yeah, I'm going. Pat's booting me out,' said Tanya.

'Come on now, Tanya. You know you were only here on a temporary basis,' said the social worker. 'And we'll work really hard to get you a new placement. Anyway, it's not so bad in this new children's home.'

'It'll be a dump,' said Tanya. 'They all are. Because they're dumping grounds. For kids nobody wants.'

'I want you, Tanya!' I said.

She gave me a sad little smile. 'Hey, I want to say goodbye to my friend,' she said to the social worker. 'How about giving us two minutes alone together, eh?'

The social worker straightened up and sighed. 'OK. *One* minute. I need to sort some stuff out with Mrs Williams anyway.'

She went out the room. Tanya and I sat together on her bed. I tried desperately hard to think of the right thing to say but there weren't any words.

'Oh, Tanya,' I said, and then I hugged her so hard I nearly knocked her over. The tin of felt-tips slid off the bed and sprinkled rainbow colours all over the carpet.

'Hey, watch it!' said Tanya. 'Now look what you've done.' She gave me a little pat and then

wriggled free. 'Let's get them all picked up. You don't want to lose any, do you? What did you bring them over for anyway? It's not like we've got time to do any colouring.'

I knelt down too, feeling for the felt-tips that had rolled under the bed.

'They're for you, Tanya,' I said. 'A goodbye present.'

'What? All of them?' said Tanya.

'Well, one or two won't be much good by themselves,' I said, giving her a little poke. 'Yes. All of them.'

'Are you sure? You can't give me your rainbow felt-tips. What will your mum say?'

'It's not up to my mum. They're mine, so it's up to me. And I want you to have them.'

'Oh, Mandy. No-one's ever given me such a lovely present,' said Tanya. She rubbed her eyes. They already looked sore, with purple shadows underneath. I didn't know if it was her make-up, or because she was so sad. But she managed another smile. 'Keep looking, there's a green and a blue still missing. I want a totally complete perfect set of felt-tip pens, thanks very much!'

We found the green and the blue and slotted them into place. Tanya ran her finger over all the pens so that they played a strange little tune.

'Mine,' she said. Then she looked round the room. She poked about in her half-full plastic bag. 'I'd better find a present for you, eh?'

'No, it's all right. Honestly. Anyway you've given me lots of stuff. The velvet scrunchie and—'

'I want to give you something special. Seeing as your rainbow felt-tips were probably your very best thing.' Tanya tipped the plastic bag up and emptied it onto the carpet. She scrabbled and then seized something triumphantly. Her violet sequin sparkly top.

'Here! You have it, Mandy.'

'But I can't. It's your special top.'

'That's why I want you to have it. My best thing for my best friend,' said Tanya.

We had one last hug.

And then we had to say goodbye.

Rainbow

I couldn't believe Tanya was gone. I kept thinking of things I had to tell her – and then remembering. Every time I heard footsteps out in the street I leapt to the window, even though I knew it couldn't possibly be her.

I couldn't settle to anything at all. I couldn't even play Miranda Rainbow. I was stuck being me, Mandy White, and I couldn't stand it.

Mum and Dad tried hard to distract me. Mum even bought me a big new tin of rainbow felt-tips without a murmur. 'It was very sweet of you to give Tanya your other set,' she said.

'You didn't even want me to say goodbye to her,' I said.

'I was still in a state of shock after having to collect you from the police,' said Mum.

'You never liked Tanya, though. You didn't ever want me to see her,' I said fiercely.

'You're being a bit hard on your mum,' said Dad. 'We only said you couldn't see her after the shoplifting business. And it's silly to say we didn't like her. She was a smashing girl in many ways, so lively, and basically good-hearted—'

'She *is*. Don't talk about her as if she's dead,' I said. 'She's still my best ever friend, you know, even though she's gone. And Mum didn't ever want us to be friends, did you?'

'Now, now,' said Mum. 'All right, I didn't think it was very sensible. And I was proved right, too. But there's no need to look at me like that, Mandy. I didn't have anything against Tanya personally. It's just that she wasn't the right age for you, and she didn't come from the right sort of background.'

'Melanie is the right age, the right background, you thought she was the right sort of friend for me. And she was ever so mean to me and ganged up with Kim and Sarah against me. They were hateful. Tanya was always lovely to me.'

I didn't just say it. I shouted it. I thought they'd get cross then. But they just stared at each other, looking helpless.

'That's a good point, Mandy,' said Dad, sighing.

'It's not as simple as that,' said Mum. 'But I

353

wish I'd tried a bit harder with Tanya.'

'It's easy to say that now, when she's been taken away,' I said.

I stamped off to my room and slammed the door. I lay on my bed for a while, clutching Olivia Orang-Utan, pretending her orange fur was Tanya's hair. Then I sat up and dressed her in Tanya's violet sequin top. It fell way past her paws, an amazing evening gown.

I tried on the top myself. I took off my glasses and peered short-sightedly into the mirror. I could just see a swirl of purple sequins. I could kid myself I looked amazingly glamorous, a real Miranda Rainbow. But then I put my glasses back on and everything shifted into focus. I was Mandy White again, and I went in and out in all the wrong places. The violet top puckered loosely over my flat chest and showed off my babyish round tummy.

'Mandy?' It was Mum, knocking at my bedroom door.

I tried to rip the top off quickly, because I couldn't stand the thought of Mum laughing at me. My head got caught and when I pulled, my glasses went flying. They fell with a clatter on my chest of drawers and broke in two again.

'Oh, no!'

'What's the matter, Mandy?' said Mum, coming in.

'My glasses! They've broken again.'

'Well, we'll see if Daddy can fix them with Superglue like he did last time. But I think we'll have to get you a new pair some time this summer,' said Mum.

'Really grown-up fashionable glasses?' I asked.

'Yes. So long as they're not too expensive.'

'And can I have my hair cut so that they won't look stupid with my baby plaits?'

'Mmm. I'm not so sure about that,' said Mum. 'If it's really important to you then maybe you can. I suppose it's your own hair after all.' Mum paused. 'But I tell you one thing I am sure about, Mandy. I don't want you wearing that purple sequin top. Certainly not outdoors.'

'It doesn't fit right, anyway,' I said. 'But it looked lovely on Tanya.'

'Well,' said Mum.

'I miss her so,' I said. 'She said she'd write,

but she hates writing, so I don't think she will.'

'I know you're missing her, darling. And I understand. But believe me, you'll make some other friends soon. Tell you what, why don't you get in touch with that nice boy who rang you up after the accident? Arthur.'

'No! I couldn't. I'd feel stupid.'

'I'll get in touch with his mother if you like.'

'No, Mum! I don't *want* to. I don't want to do anything,' I insisted.

Dad took time off work and kept suggesting we go to the pictures or the park. He spent one day taking me round the museums in London and I pretended I was enjoying myself – but I'd have been just as happy lying on my bed at home doing nothing.

Mum scoured the local newspaper for holiday activities and eventually talked me into signing up for a story-writing session at the library.

She took me shopping on Saturday and said I could have new glasses. I tried on hundreds of pairs: tiny owly ones, great big bold specs, glittery party glasses. I wished Tanya was there to tell me which suited me most. Mum liked a baby pink pair with a little white rabbit at either end. I knew I never wanted to wear anything with a rabbit on it ever again. Particularly in pink.

'But pink suits you so, Mandy,' said Mum.

'Not pink, Mum. Any other colour. Red. Orange. Purple.'

I peered through glasses all the colours of the rainbow. And then I spotted a perfect pair. Not too little. Not too large. With striped frames. Rainbow stripes. Red, orange, yellow, green, blue, indigo, violet.

'Oh, Mum! I like these best. Can I have the rainbow glasses?'

They weren't too expensive so Mum said yes. We went and had an ice cream in Maxwell's while we were waiting for my glasses to be made up with the right lenses for me. I chose a strawberry special, sprinkled with rainbow dots. Mum had one too, even though she was supposed to be on another diet.

'I wish I'd taken Tanya here now,' said Mum.

We finished our strawberry specials in silence.

Mum decided to chance going into work late the next Monday so she could deliver me at the library for the writing session. She wanted to come in with me but I wouldn't let her, in case any of the children thought me a baby.

I needn't have worried. There was only one other person my age. Arthur!

He was already sitting at a table at the back of the room with two other boys. There wasn't a spare chair at his table. And I didn't want him to think I was being pushy. He didn't seem all that thrilled to see me there. He just nodded nervously at me, going pink.

I didn't want to embarrass him further in front of the other boys. They were maybe his friends.

I didn't know who to sit with. I didn't want to squash up with the very little ones printing in wobbly wax crayon.

There were two girls about seven at another table.

'Maybe you'd like to sit with Sarah and Julie and work on their Woodland Bunny story with them?' said the library lady.

'No, thank you,' I said. 'I don't really want to write about rabbits. I'll make up my own story.'

I sat at a little table by myself. The library lady offered me paper and pencils and wax crayons, but I had my own drawing book and my new tin of rainbow felt-tips with me. Arthur was looking at me so I hurriedly started writing. I didn't want him to think I was trying to catch his eye.

I wrote down the special story Tanya and I had made up together, about Love Tanyanita and Miranda Rainbow sharing a flat together. It made me feel very lonely and sad remembering it. I kept hearing Tanya's voice as she made it all up.

'Are you all right, Mandy?' the library lady asked, bending over me.

'Yes, I'm fine,' I said, feeling stupid. I put my arm over my page. I didn't want her to read our private story.

She moved on to the boys' table at the back. The boys who weren't Arthur were scribbling stories based on video games. They'd got a bit bored and were flicking rubbers at each other, going Zap and Pow and Kerplunk. The library lady sighed and skirted round them towards Arthur.

'What are you writing today, Arthur?' she said, smiling expectantly. Arthur was obviously a regular at the story-writing sessions.

The Zap-Pow-Kerplunk boys rolled their eyes and made gagging gestures.

'It's nothing. It's just . . . No, honestly,' Arthur mumbled.

'"The Knight Who Wouldn't Fight",' the library lady read out loud.

'The knight who wouldn't fight!' said Zap.

'What a dumb wimpy title,' said Pow.

'By a dumb wimpy boy,' said Zap.

'Dumb, wimpy, nitty-Knighty Arthur,' said Pow.

'Now then, you two, stop being so silly,' said the library lady. 'Don't take any notice of them, Arthur.'

Arthur said nothing. He didn't look at the boys. He didn't look at the library lady. He didn't look at me.

I looked at him properly through my new rainbow glasses. Then I got up and walked over to his table.

'Can I see what you've written, Arthur?' I said. 'Here, I bet those two haven't even heard of King Arthur and all the knights of the round table. They're still way down at the Super Mario and Sonic stage.'

Zap and Pow spluttered and squealed. The library lady blinked. Arthur went bright red. But he pushed his book towards me.

'Here,' he said. He sounded gruff. But I knew it was OK.

I got my chair and sat at his table for a bit, but Zap and Pow kept bombarding us with rubbers and jogging us whenever we wrote, so Arthur and I moved over to my little table.

I decided I wanted to go to the story-writing sessions all week. Arthur and I sat together every day. We started to work on a new story together, about a beautiful medieval witch, Mandiana the Magic, and an all-powerful wizard called Dark Art. We took turns writing the story and drew a picture for every page and coloured it all in with my rainbow felt-tips.

I knew that Arthur was pleased I'd turned up at the library out of the blue. He hadn't said much because he was shy, like me. He didn't want me to think *he* was pushy.

Arthur's mum came to meet him at lunchtimes. She studied in the library archives while we did our writing class. She had the same pale face and untidy fringe as Arthur. They even wore identical navy anoraks. She was a different sort of mum but ever so interesting when you talked to her. She gave us some brilliant ideas for evil spells and knew all about poisonous potions and herbs.

My mum got on well with Arthur's mum. They made friends too. Arthur's mum said I was very welcome to go round to their house in the mornings when the writing sessions stopped.

'That would be good, eh, Mandy?' said Arthur, going pink again.

'Yeah. Right,' I said.

It wouldn't be as good as being with Tanya of course. Nowhere near. But Arthur was OK. He was a friend.

But I didn't go to the Kings' house the next week after all.

I knew something terrible had happened when Mum came to collect me on Friday. Her eyes were red and her face was all puffy. My tummy went tight.

'Mum, what's wrong?'

She tried hard to be brave in front of Mrs King and Arthur.

'Nothing's really wrong, dear. I've just had a little shock, that's all.'

'Have you heard something awful about Tanya?'

Mum stared at me as if I was mad.

'No, of course not. No, I've just been forced to join the massed ranks of the unemployed,' said Mum.

She was talking in such a strange way I didn't get what she meant at first. But then when Mrs King started talking very sympathetically about redundancy I realized. Mum had lost her job.

When we were indoors, away from the Kings, her face went wobbly and she started crying again.

'Don't cry, Mum,' I said timidly.

She cried harder, her eyes screwed up, her mouth open. I'd never seen her cry that way before. It made me feel awful and embarrassed and scared.

Mum went up to her bedroom and I hung back for a minute and then followed her worriedly. She'd taken her good suit off and was lying on top of her duvet in her petticoat, crying and crying.

'Mum?' I said, and I sat down gingerly on the edge of the bed.

I reached out and patted her soft, shaking shoulder.

'Oh, Mandy,' Mum sobbed, and then she scrabbled around for a hankie and tried hard to stop crying. 'I'm sorry, darling. Don't look so worried. It's not the end of the world. I don't know why I'm making such a fuss.' Her voice wavered up and down, and every so often there was a sob she couldn't stop, like a hiccup.

'You'll get another job, Mum,' I said.

Mum shook her head. 'I'm not so sure, Mandy. Oh dear, it was so awful. I had to clear my desk and get out straightaway. I couldn't believe it was really happening. Everyone looked at me as if I'd got some horrible disease. My boss said it was because I was unreliable. He kept on about all the time off I'd had, what with my teeth playing up and then when I had to look after you—'

'So it's my fault?' I said.

'No, no! Of course not, Mandy. And anyway, he was just using that as an excuse. He practically admitted it. He said I didn't really fit into a busy modern office. My way of thinking was all wrong. He said I was too old-fashioned. But what he really meant was that I was too *old*.'

'Oh, Mum. You're not old. Well. Not *that* old.'

'Yes, I am,' said Mum. She blew her nose and sat up properly. 'Goodness, I must look a sight. I *am* old, Mandy. When I look at the other mums down at your school I can't help realizing I'm old enough to be *their* mum.'

'You're not anyone else's mum but mine,' I said, and I put my arms round her.

Mum went after lots of jobs that summer but for a long time she kept getting turned down. She got very depressed and she even started to get thinner, because she didn't feel like eating much. I'd always longed for Mum to stop being so fat, but now I wasn't sure. It was as if the Mum I knew was slowly wearing away, like a bar of soap. I wanted her really big and really bossy again, because that was the way she was supposed to be.

But it was OK after all. The week before I started back at school Mum got another job. She'd gone after an office job in Maxwell's, but she hadn't been able to cope with their computer. They suggested she apply as one of their part-time sales staff instead. She got a job going in Ladies' Separates, and she took me for enormous knickerbocker glories in Maxwell's soda fountain to celebrate.

'It's a lovely department. I like the look of the ladies I'll be working with. It's less money, but I'll get a good discount on goods, even though I'm only part-time,' said Mum, licking ice cream from her lips and scraping her tall glass. 'Pity I don't get discounts on ice creams, eh?'

Mum was happy again. I wished I could feel happy too. I still missed Tanya so much. I had Arthur now, but he wasn't the same. And school was starting on Monday, and I'd begun to have nightmares about Kim and Melanie and Sarah.

I kept telling myself it was a new school year, a new class, a new start. But I still felt sick and sweaty when I walked into school. Kim and Melanie and Sarah were already in the classroom, at the back. Kim whispered something and they all burst out laughing, looking at me.

It was starting again. I stood still, not knowing where to sit. All the girls had friends already. I was stuck without anyone.

Arthur was sitting right at the front. He tapped the desk next to him.

'Hey, Mandy. Come and sit here,' he said.

I stared at him. None of the girls ever sat with the boys. You just never did it, not in our class.

'I can't sit next to you, Arthur,' I hissed 'You're a boy.'

'Brilliant deduction!'

said Arthur, raising his eyebrows. 'So what?'

I thought about it. So what, indeed? I sat next to Arthur. Kim and Melanie and Sarah giggled and sneered. Some of the boys wolf-whistled and made stupid remarks.

'Nutters,' said Arthur.

'Nutters,' I agreed.

'They're the nutty ones,' said Kim. 'Two swotty little twits. They're just sticking together because they haven't got any other friends.'

She went on and on, but her words were just like little pinpricks, not great big daggers. I knew it wasn't true. I did have friends. I had Tanya, who was the best friend in all the world. And I had Arthur.

We stayed sitting together at the front, and the new Year Six teacher Miss Moseley didn't mind at all.

Kim and Melanie and Sarah sat in a three-some at the back, all crammed together. Miss Moseley wasn't having any of that.

'Come on, you three. You haven't got room to work all squashed up like that. One of you had better pop over to a spare table.'

Melanie and Sarah looked at Kim pleadingly, both desperate to stay with her. Kim sat back, smiling, looking from one to the other. We all craned round to see who she was going to pick and who she was going to send packing.

'Kim?' said Miss Moseley. She knew her name already. Everyone in the whole school knew Kim. 'You go and sit at the spare table, please.'

We all stared at Miss Moseley, astonished. She didn't understand. Or maybe she understood all too well.

'No, I'll stay here,' said Kim. 'Melanie can sit at the spare table. Or Sarah.'

Melanie and Sarah looked agonized.

'I want to stay with you, Kim,' said Melanie.

'No, I've got to stay, I've been your friend much longer,' said Sarah.

'It's not up to Kim,' said Miss Moseley briskly. 'I'm the teacher and I say who sits where. Melanie and Sarah, stay where you are. Kim. You move to the spare table.' She paused.
'At once!'

Kim got to her feet and moved all her things to the spare table. She had two bright pink spots on her cheeks. She glared at Miss Moseley.

Miss Moseley smiled. 'Right. Now we're all sorted out and sitting comfortably, we can start our lesson.'

We were all still a bit stunned. Miss Moseley was young with fluffy fair hair and she often wore fluffy pastel jumpers. We'd thought she was all soft and fluffy too. We'd got it wrong. She was as strong as steel.

I decided I was going to like it in Year Six with Miss Moseley. We started all sorts of new lessons. We were doing the Victorians all that first term and we all had to choose one special aspect to study with a partner. Arthur and I decided to do a project about this group of Victorian painters who liked doing pictures of King Arthur and all his knights and various damsels in distress. The others in the class chose stuff like Childhood or Servants or Fashion or Railways. Miss Moseley was very pleased with Arthur and me. She said we'd started a very original and interesting project.

Kim made vomit noises. Miss Moseley raised her eyebrows but she didn't bother to get cross. She didn't seem to think Kim was particularly important.

We had one brand new subject in Year Six. It was down on our timetable for Friday afternoon. It was called Circle Time. We weren't quite sure what it was.

'Maybe we'll draw circles with protractors,' said Arthur, getting his protractor out of his pencil case.

'What, to make patterns? I like doing that,' I said. 'And then we can colour them in.'

But we didn't draw circles in Circle Time. We made the circle ourselves, pushing the tables back and sitting round on our chairs. Miss Moseley sat in the circle too. Kim could sit in between Melanie and Sarah again. She barged between them. Arthur and I sat next to each other of course.

'Circle Time is going to be our special time, when we sit round together as a class and talk about all sorts of different things,' said Miss Moseley.

'Oooh, she's going to tell us about sex,' said Kim, and everyone giggled.

Miss Moseley laughed too.

'Not today, folks. So you can all simmer down. Circle Time is when we discuss various issues.'

'What's an issue, Miss Moseley?'

'Issue! Issue!' said Kim, pretending to sneeze.

'An issue is something currently on our minds. Something we want to talk about . . .'

'Like *Neighbours*?'

'No, not exactly. But all sorts of issues are dealt with in *Neighbours*. Anyway. Today in Circle Time I thought we'd talk about bullying,' said Miss Moseley.

There was a sudden silence. Everyone looked

at Kim. Her cheeks went pink with the Dutch doll spots. People were looking at Melanie and Sarah too. And me. I started to feel sick. I didn't want to talk about it. And if Kim and Melanie and Sarah got told off they'd think I'd been telling tales on them. I stared at Miss Moseley. She was going to make it worse.

But Miss Moseley smiled at me, smiled at everyone, calm and composed, her fair hair standing out around her face like a golden halo. She took out a newspaper and read to us about a boy who had been beaten up by three other boys at his school. She showed us the photo of his poor bruised face. We all agreed that this was awful. Then she read to us about a girl who kept getting punched and kicked until she was so scared of going to school that she hanged herself. We discussed this too. Miss Moseley asked us to think how the boy and girl must have felt. It started to get really sad and scary.

'I don't want to think about that girl hanging herself. It'll give me nightmares,' said Melanie.

'I know it's very uncomfortable thinking about it. But you're all getting older and much more sensible now you're in Year Six. You're ready to discuss very painful grown-up topics. Now, what do you all think we should do about bullies like this?'

'They should get beaten up, too.'

'They should get locked up.'

'No-one should ever talk to them ever again.'

People's suggestions started to get fiercer and fiercer.

'This isn't always possible, or indeed practical,' said Miss Moseley. 'And I think we have to try to work out *why* people bully. Then we can maybe stop it before it gets too much of a habit. So. Why do *you* think people bully?'

'Because they're big and they want to hurt.'

'Because they're nasty.'

'Because they like getting people scared.'

'Yes. These are all sensible suggestions. But try to think a bit deeper. Are bullies happy people?' Miss Moseley asked.

'They're happy when they hurt.'

'Yes, I suppose so. But think about it. Think about when you're very very happy. Say it's your birthday and all your family and friends

have given you a big hug and some lovely presents and you feel really great. Now. Do you
want to hurt anyone when you're in that sort of
situation?'

We thought – and shook our heads.

'Of course not. You just want to be nice to
people. But suppose you've had a really bad day
and got into trouble at school and your friend's
gone off with someone else and your mum and
dad are cross and they've given your little sister
a treat and yet they just tell you off . . . Do you
want to be nice to people now? Or do you feel
like being nasty?'

'Nasty!' we said.

'Of course you do. So if your little sister
comes and starts showing off, you maybe give
her a little push, or tell her she's stupid, right?'

Most people nodded, laughing.

'But that's not real bullying. I mean, I can't
stick *my* sister, but I wouldn't kick her head in
or make her kill herself.'

People laughed more, but Miss Moseley was
looking serious.

'That's exactly it, though. Bullying isn't
always terribly dramatic and dreadful, with
people seriously hurt or even dying. We're all
very thankful nothing like that happens in our
school. But I'm sure we can all think of various
occasions when a group of us have picked on
another one?'

No-one was laughing now. My tummy went tight again.

'One person gets picked on, and it starts to be a habit. And others join in. Because everyone wants to side with the bully so that *they* don't get picked on.'

'Sometimes they ask for it. Because they're *stupid*,' someone muttered. It could have been Kim.

Miss Moseley had very sharp ears under her fluffy hair.

'No-one ever asks to be bullied,' she said. 'But you're right, sometimes people get bullied because they're stupid. Though that's not a very kind word. People can't help it if they're not very bright. And that's a terrible reason for bullying someone, just because they're not clever.'

'And other times someone can get bullied because they're *ever* so clever,' Arthur said suddenly. 'Say they come top of the class and the bully doesn't like it because they're clever too and *they* want to be top.'

Miss Moseley nodded.

'That's very shrewd of you, Arthur.'

Some of the others were whispering and nudging each other. I heard the word Kim several times. And Mandy.

'We won't mention any names,' said Miss

Moseley. 'Remember, this is a *general* discussion.'

Melanie and Sarah were fidgeting. Kim's cheeks were strawberry pink.

'If someone is being bullied you should always tell,' said Miss Moseley, her eyes swivelling round the whole circle. 'Tell your mum and dad. Tell your teacher. Tell another teacher if things still don't get sorted out. The person who is getting bullied needs help. And the person doing the bullying needs help too, because they're sad, sick, silly people. We should feel sorry for them, even though they hurt and do a lot of harm. Even name-calling and silly teasing can be horribly upsetting, can't it?' She looked round the circle again. 'You know what I mean. Pulling silly faces and going chitter-chatter, like a lot of monkeys at the zoo. Bullies are like baboons, those big monkeys with weird faces and bright red bottoms.'

Everyone burst out laughing hearing Miss Moseley say the word bottom.

'The biggest baboon screams a lot and bites all the little ones. All the other big baboons copy, screeching and scratching for fleas. Now, no-one here in my class wants to act like a bully baboon with a bright red bottom, do they?'

Everyone shook their heads – even Melanie and Sarah. Kim's head was bent.

She kept right out of my way after that. She didn't ever wait to get me after school again. She'd have been by herself anyway. Melanie and Sarah didn't want to be her friend any more. They went round just the two of them instead.

Melanie asked if I wanted to make friends again. I said OK but I couldn't be her *best* friend. I had Arthur now anyway. We stayed sitting together in school and we played together in the dinner break and we always walked home together as far as the bus stop. Mum still came to meet me most days, but I didn't mind now that no-one teased me about it.

I still couldn't help hoping that somehow one day Tanya might come running down the road too, in her shorts and clacky sandals. I'd heard from her at last. Just one postcard, and she hadn't put an address.

Hi Mandy
    I sed Id rit. The Juv. Cort was a dodel. I jest got a soopervison order. Grat, eh? And I think Im geting a new foster Mum so things are luking up.
    See you, best frend.
    Lots of lov
    Tanya x x x

See you. I had to keep hoping that I really would see her again some day. If she didn't come back to see me then I'd simply have to go looking for her when I was a bit older. We were still best ever friends. We had to meet up again. Somewhere . . .

ABOUT THE AUTHOR

JACQUELINE WILSON was born in Bath in 1945, but has spent most of her life in Kingston-upon-Thames, Surrey. She always wanted to be a writer and wrote her first 'novel' when she was nine, filling countless Woolworths' exercise books as she grew up. She started work at a publishing company and then went on to work as a journalist on *Jackie* magazine (which was named after her) before turning to writing fiction full-time.

Since 1990 Jacqueline has written prolifically for children and has won many of the UK's top awards for children's books, including the Smarties Prize in 2000 and the Guardian Children's Fiction Award and the Children's Book of the Year in 1999. Jacqueline was awarded an OBE in the Queen's Birthday Honours list, in Golden Jubilee Year, 2002.

Over 10 million copies of Jacqueline's books have now been sold in the UK and approximately 50,000 copies of her book are sold each month. An avid reader herself, Jacqueline has a personal collection of more than 15,000 books.

She has one grown-up daughter.

'A brilliant young writer of wit and subtlety whose stories are never patronising and are often complex and many-layered'
THE TIMES

'Jacqueline Wilson has a rare gift for writing lightly and amusingly about emotional issues'
BOOKSELLER

'Wilson writes like a child, and children instantly recognize themselves in her characters. The tone of voice is faultless, her stories are about the problems many children face, and her plots work with classic simplicity . . . a subtle art is concealed by artlessness and some might call that genius'
DAILY TELEGRAPH

THE BED AND BREAKFAST STAR

Jacqueline Wilson

Where do baby apes sleep?
In apricots!

I'm Elsa, and that's one of my jokes (I tell *lots*
of jokes and I'm going to be a big star one day).
I do my best to cheer my family up – but no-one
seems to laugh much any more. Not since we lost
our lovely house and had to move into a bed and
breakfast hotel ...

'Written with characteristic verve'
JUNIOR EDUCATION

ISBN 0-440-86324-4

Now available from all good book stores

CORGI YEARLING BOOKS

THE STORY OF TRACY BEAKER
Jacqueline Wilson

*I'm Tracy Beaker. This is a book all
about me. I'd read it if were you.
It's the most incredible dynamic
heart-rending story. Honest.*

Tracy is ten years old. She lives in a Children's
Home but would like a real home one day, with
a real family. Meet Tracy, follow her story, and
share her hopes for the future in this beautifully
observed, touching, and often very funny tale,
all told in Tracy's own words.

*'Both entertaining and moving. A book that
lingers in the mind long after it is put down'*
THE GUARDIAN

*'Sit up and take notice, here comes the female
counterpart of Adrian Mole and I wouldn't
mind betting she will be as popular'*
THE SCHOOL LIBRARIAN

ISBN 0-440-86279-5

Now available from all good book stores
CORGI YEARLING BOOKS

THE SUITCASE KID
Jacqueline Wilson

When my parents split up they didn't
know what to do with me ...

My family always lived at Mulberry Cottage. Mum,
Dad, me – and Radish, my Sylvanian rabbit. But now
mum lives with Bill the Baboon and his three kids.
Dad lives with Carrie and her twins. And where do
I live? I live out of a suitcase. One week with Mum's
new family, one week with Dad's.

It's as easy as ABC. That's what everyone says.
But all I want is to go home – back to Mulberry Cottage ...

Meet ten-year-old Andy and share her
experiences of life after divorce in this
realistic, moving, yet often funny tale.

'Honest, angry, sometimes sad and always very readable'
THE TIMES EDUCATIONAL SUPPLEMENT

ISBN 0-440-86311-2

Now available from all good book stores

CORGI YEARLING BOOKS

THE LOTTIE PROJECT
Jacqueline Wilson

I don't want to d a boring old project,
Who wants to be like everyone else's? I'm
doing a diary . . .

Hi! I'm Charlie (DON'T call me Charlotte – ever!)
History is boring, right? Wrong! The Victorians
weren't all deadly dull and drippy. *Lottie* certainly
isn't. She's eleven – like me – but she's left school
and has a job as a nursery maid. Her life is really
hard, just work, work, work, but I bet *she'd* know
what to do about my mum's awful boyfriend and his
wimpy little son. I bet she wouldn't mess it all up like
I do . . .

'Vivid, superbly observed story of real life'
THE TIMES

ISBN 0-440-86366-X

Now available from all good book stores

CORGI YEARLING BOOKS